I0690567

THE TALES OF
RICK AND ALEC

First Edition

Published by The Nazca Plains Corporation
Las Vegas, Nevada
2011

ISBN: 978-1-61098-209-2
E-book: 978-1-61098-210-8

Published by

The Nazca Plains Corporation ®
4640 Paradise Rd, Suite 141
Las Vegas NV 89109-8000

PUBLISHER'S NOTE
The Tales of Rick and Alec is a work of fiction created wholly by Hank
Brooks' imagination. All characters are fictional and any resemblance
to any persons living or deceased is purely by accident. No portion of
this book reflects any real person or events.

Cover Photo, Joel Benjamin
Cover Design, Scott Ian Ray
Art Director, Blake Stephens

THE TALES OF RICK AND ALEC

First Edition

Hank Brooks

DEDICATION

To all the downtrodden who never lose hope.

CONTENTS

THE TALES OF RICK AND ALEC

THE TALES OF THE COUNTRY CLUB

THE TALES OF RICK AND ALEC

Tale One: Under The Bridge

Even when the lad had everything that he wanted, he had heard about the bridges.

A river bisected his small city in Northern Maine. Two bridges spanned the river, one at the north end and one at the south end of the city. Slowly, over the past decade, homeless wretches had begun to live under the bridges. Little by little, make-shift tent cities had grown under each bridge, and it was common to see small fires at night, where food was being cooked and frigid fingers were warmed. Every so often, at the urgings of the citizens, the police had removed the inhabitants of the tent cities, given them a night's shelter in jail, and demolished their makeshift shelters. Now six months after his eighteenth birthday, Rick found himself one of the homeless. Hungry and cold, he had gravitated toward the south bridge. Subconsciously the word south sounded warmer than the word north.

He had no tent to shelter him, so he huddled as close as he could to any fire still burning. He had tried to find some work, but who would hire him? He was dirty and disheveled. He had no money for new clothes, and no means to wash what he was wearing. He was sure he stunk, but so did the fellow human beings around him. Some of the other unfortunate souls under the bridge were kind enough to dole out what little food they could spare to help keep the boy alive. His once robust body was shriveling away.

He had been living under the south bridge for nearly two months. He had learned to fall asleep no matter how cold it was, and no matter how much noise there was around him. This night he had propped himself up against a bridge piling. His ass was frozen from the concrete it was sitting on. He covered himself with a tattered blanket that he had found in someone's garbage. Ever since he had obtained the blanket, he felt that he was sleeping luxuriously. In minutes he was fast asleep and he began to dream. He dreamed he was back home.

He was in his back yard. The ground was covered with colorful autumn leaves. He and his younger brother had raked the lawn less than forty-eight hours ago, but it was fully covered again. It was Friday afternoon, and the boys promised their father they would rake again on Saturday. The days had grown short and they were afraid they could not complete the job before it got dark if they started raking after school. Their father reluctantly grunted his assent. The two boys were tossing around a baseball. They were both very athletically inclined.

The scene shifted. He was standing in the front door on that same night. He was waving goodbye to his kid brother who was walking up the street for a sleepover at his friend's house. His parents were just pulling out of the driveway, headed for a meeting at their church. They told him that they would not be home before midnight and he should be sure to be asleep when they got home. No sooner did his parents' car turn the corner, then his best friend Peter ran up to the door. He and Rick went into the house and locked the door behind them.

They bounded upstairs to Rick's bedroom. Nobody was home and they didn't bother to shut the door. The two young men shed their clothing in record time and fell into each other's arms. Two erect cocks ground together and each of them moaned in delight. Their tongues dueled inside their mouths. Still locked together they made their way to the bed and lay down on top of the covers.

They twisted into a sixty-nine position immediately, and went to work. They were too young and too horny for any kind of preliminaries. They both knew that they wouldn't last long and neither of them attempted to prolong their orgasms. They came seconds apart, and swallowed their juices greedily. Peter's head was facing the footboard, and when he felt Rick's cock softening, he released it and climbed up to lie beside his lover. They began to kiss and fondle each other immediately. Their fingers played with each other's ass holes. After a few minutes of fingering each other, Rick told Peter to lie on his stomach. Peter happily obliged. He was aware of what was coming. They both knew that eventually they would fuck each other, but it hadn't happened yet. Nevertheless they played an anal game, and both their cocks began to rise in anticipation.

When Peter lay prone on his stomach, Rick mounted him. He began to nibble on Peter's ears and then on his neck. Rick's body slipped down Peter's body in slow motion. As he descended, he kissed and nibbled all over Peter's back. At last he reached his prize; Peter's bubbly butt. He placed a palm on each cheek and began to knead it. Then he began to kiss both cheeks and he ran his tongue all over them. Finally he spread the cheeks and placed his tongue directly on Peter's crack. He began to slather all over Peter's butt hole. Soon he made his tongue as hard and as sharp as possible, and pushed it as far into Peter's asshole as he could. Peter was twisting and writhing beneath Rick's tongue. He was moaning loudly.

"Don't stop," he begged. "You're killing me. Please don't stop."

They were so lost in passion that neither of them heard the front door open.

A committee of five couples was to assemble that night with their minister to plan a special Thanksgiving Service. When Rick's parents arrived at the church nobody was there and the door to the meeting room was locked. They were perplexed, but waited about ten minutes before Rick's dad got out his cell phone and called

Pastor Harding. He asked the pastor where everyone was. Listening carefully, he pulled out his appointment book from his hip pocket. It distinctly listed the meeting for tonight, but the good pastor explained that the meeting was scheduled for the following Friday night. Red faced, they returned home.

There was no mistaking the noises they heard when they opened the front door. They had a very active sex life, and they knew the sounds of love when they heard it. Rick's dad was not certain what to do. Of course, he assumed that his son was fucking some nubile young girl, and the man in him didn't want to confront that situation until it was over. The couple was curious and listened as hard as they could, hoping they would recognize the girl's voice. It didn't take them long to realize that they were hearing two male voices.

The blood rose up in Rick's dad's face. His hands clenched involuntarily into hard fists, and he bounded up the stairs in time to see his elder son and heir sucking some other guy's ass.

"Stop, godamyou," he yelled. He grabbed his son around the neck and threw him to the floor. Neither boy knew what hit him. Peter grabbed his clothes and ran out of the house. Fortunately for him, Rick's dad did not recognize him.

"Get dressed before your mother sees you," he bellowed, "and then get out of my house." Fifteen minutes later, Rick was out on the street, never to see his home again. He didn't have a dime in his pocket, and his only protection from the weather was a light windbreaker. He did not dare to contact Peter. His only thought was to protect his lover.

His reveries were rudely interrupted, and he was brought back to reality by someone shaking his shoulder. He opened his eyes to see another man more scrungy than he was. He had on a shirt and jeans that were in good condition, but they were easily as dirty as his own. He was wearing sneakers without socks. He was wrapped in a blanket.

Rick instinctively turned his head away. The man's body odor was totally offensive, but then Rick realized that he probably smelled as bad. He looked into the man's face. It was covered by at least a month's growth of blond hair and it was impossible for Rick to make out the guy's age or if he was plain, handsome or in between. In spite of his misery, Rick was impressed at the man's package straining at his tight jeans.

"What do you want?" Rick asked in a husky voice which was no longer used to conversation.

The man hesitated before speaking. "I have seen you here for days," he started to say. His voice was soft and kind. Rick relaxed a bit. The man pointed to a tent a few feet away.

"That's my shelter," he said. "It's big enough for two. You're freezing to death. Would you like to share it with me? It will be tight, but our body heat will also help to warm things up."

Rick stared at the man a long time without answering. He wanted to do as the man asked, but he was frankly frightened. Then he wondered what he had to be afraid of. He was penniless and his life was worthless.

Finally, the man broke the uncomfortable silence. "I mean you no harm," he said. "You would be doing me a favor also. I'm so lonely. Frankly it would be nice to touch another human being." That having been said, he reached out to touch Rick's face, but Rick recoiled.

"I'm sorry," the man said as he turned away to leave.

"Wait," Rick called after him. "If the offer is still open, I'd like to share your shelter."

The man smiled and said, "That's wonderful." He walked over to his tent and opened up the flap. Rick gathered up his blanket and followed him. The man held open the flap and Rick entered first. It would be a tight squeeze, he thought. Then he smiled. A sleeping bag covered the floor of the shelter, guarding the inhabitant from the cold concrete below. In the corner Rick could see at least one blanket, maybe two. He entered the tent and crawled to one corner, making as much room for his new friend as he could.

The man entered and sat down on the sleeping bag. There was barely enough room for the two of them. The man closed the tent flap and secured it with a string. It was pitch black inside.

"We can stretch out on the sleeping bag," he said, "and use the blankets for cover. If it won't gross you out, we can both squeeze into the sleeping bag. It will be tight but it will be the warmest way to spend the night. We can use the blankets also, of course."

Just thinking of spending a warm night was motivation enough for Rick. "I'd prefer to settle down inside the bag," he said.

Rick couldn't see in the dark, but if he could, he would have seen the man smiling. They both wiggled into the sleeping bag, and pulled the zipper halfway up. They maneuvered the blankets on top of them and closed the zipper almost all the way up to their necks. They started out lying side by side, but it was awfully tight and they instinctively turned toward each other to make more room in the sleeping bag. That's when they felt each other's erections.

"Nice," the man said, but Rick remained silent for awhile. He realized that they were both rubbing their cocks together. After a long silence, Rick seemed to find his voice.

"My name is Rick," he said. "What's yours?"

"Alec," The man said simply, and Rick felt Alec's hand cover his crotch through his jeans. He reached down and cupped Alec's package also, and they both fell asleep like that.

Rick slept well all night for the first time in weeks. He was awakened by the early morning light. He panicked when he realized that Alec was not there. The flap was not secured and so Rick peeked outside. He couldn't see Alec but he could hear him peeing behind the tent. He needed to do the same. In a moment they were peeing side by side and smiling at each other. They were not shy about letting the other guy see that they were checking each other out.

Back in the tent, Alec secured the flap and reached into a paper bag. He retrieved a hard boiled egg and a small bottle of water. The bottle was half empty. Rick could only wonder where they came from. Alec peeled the egg and threw the shell into the bag. He took a pen knife out of his pocket and cut the egg in half. He offered one half to Rick.

Rick tried to eat the egg slowly, but he was so hungry, he gobbled it up. Alec unscrewed the cap from the water bottle and handed it to Rick, who quickly washed down the egg. Alec took a swig also. He carefully recapped the bottle and put it into the bag.

"I'll dump the shell later," he said. With breakfast behind them, Alec lay down on his back. Rick lay down beside him. They were silent for awhile and then Alec said, "My name is Alec Thomas. My mother died when I was two, and it's always been me and my dad. He was my only family. He never remarried, and he did his best to raise me alone. He had no education, and he relied on laborers' jobs whenever he could get one. We never had much of anything, but we were great buddies, and managed to get along. When I was 14, my dad was killed by a crane that collapsed at a job he had snagged. They put me in foster care, but the first night I was there, my foster father came into my room and raped me. When he left the room, I ran away. I didn't want to go back to foster care so I've been living here for five years hiding from the authorities. I'm too old now for foster care, but I stay here out of habit."

Again they lay in silence. Finally Rick said. "My name is Rick Norton. I was due to graduate from high school this June. But a couple of months ago, my dad caught me having sex with another guy. Less than fifteen minutes later, I was out on the streets, without a penny and scantily dressed. I tried to get any kind of job, but as the days went by, and I got more and more messed up, my chances grew slimmer and slimmer. Does it bother you that I am gay?"

"Don't be a nerd," Alec said. 'Didn't you feel me massaging your cock last night?" Before Rick could answer, Alec leaned over and planted a foul kiss on Rick's mouth, just as his hand found Rick's crotch. Rick was instantly aroused and reached for Alec's cock.

"Not here," Alec said. He sat up and reached for something in the corner of the tent. Rick hadn't seen it before, but it was a guitar case. It had been hidden by Alec's blankets. Alec removed the guitar and started strumming it. He began to sing a country song, and Rick was amazed. His playing was fairly accomplished, but his voice was spectacular. Rick thought it was better than any voice he had ever heard on American Idol. He was speechless.

"I've been playing on street corners for years," Alec said. "It's too cold right now. Nobody wants to stop to listen to me. Anyhow, over the years, I have squirreled away enough money to get out of here. My plan is to go down south. I want to go all the way to Key

West, and never be cold again. Maybe I can get a job singing in a club, or on a cruise ship. I have no education and I'll do whatever I can. But it ain't gonna happen unless I get cleaned up and buy some clothes. I can do that now, but I never wanted to travel south alone. I need a companion to share the journey with me."

"It sounds wonderful," Rick said. Alec stared at Rick.

"You sure are dense," he said. "I'm asking you to go with me. It damn well beats freezing under a bridge."

"You want me to go with you," Rick stammered in disbelief. "Hell yeah!" he screamed and this time he leaned over to kiss Alec.

"That's fantastic," Alec said, "I have planned this for a long time so listen to me. This morning we are packing up our camp, and heading for the YMCA. I have the money for a room. We can shower and shave and look decent. Then we can buy some jeans and a few shirts and a jacket for you. I know a couple of thrift shops that will be our salvation, and shopping there will help out some other poor unfortunates. We'll have a real dinner for a change and sleep in a clean bed." Alec suddenly smiled. "Well maybe we won't sleep too much," he said. "In the morning we'll have a good breakfast and head for the bus terminal. To save money, we'll buy tickets to some place in Georgia or North Florida. From there we can walk and hitch hike and camp out. If we're lucky I can make a few bucks singing along the way."

Alec had to stop talking. It was hard for him to curb his enthusiasm, but Rick was sobbing. Alec put his arms around him. "Why are you crying?" he asked. "Aren't you as excited about this as I am?"

"Yes, yes," Rick answered. "I'm crying because I'm so fucking happy."

The desk clerk at the Y was reluctant to give them a room, but Alec laid the money on the counter and smiled at the desk clerk. "I swear," he told the man, "After we shave and clean up, you'll think that Joe College checked in." The clerk had to smile at that. There was something about Alec's soothing voice that intrigued him.

"OK," he said. "Don't disappoint me. I'll see you later."

The shower was down the hall. The two young men stripped in their room. They each had a toothbrush and a razor they had somehow managed to acquire, and Alec had shaving cream and toothpaste in his knapsack. They wrapped towels around themselves and headed for the showers.

Their first stop was at the sinks. They shaved themselves clean, and looked at each other in the mirror.

"You are so handsome," Rick said.

"And you are more handsome than my dad was," Alec answered. "I secretly had desires for him, and have always regretted that I never seduced him. He might have liked that."

"Shut up. You're making me hot. Look." Rick pointed at his seven inch, cut boner.

Alec pointed at his slightly larger uncut boner. "Brush your teeth," he ordered. "I'm saving it for later, after we have done all our shopping and our errands."

It was hard for them not to touch each other in the shower. They lingered for what seemed forever, enjoying the warm water, and cleansing themselves of weeks of accumulated grime. When they were finished, they returned to their room. They gathered up every bit of dirty laundry they had and headed to the laundry room wrapped in towels. Along the way they passed some other roomers who stared appreciatively.

Alec had brought along some dollar bills. He put one in a machine and was rewarded with quarters for the appliances. Another machine offered laundry detergent. Alec got the wash started and said to Rick, "I really want to wait until later when we don't have to rush, so I'll go back to our room and you stay with the wash. I'll come back in forty-five minutes and stay while it dries." He gave Rick a chaste kiss on the lips and left Rick with his towel tenting.

In less than two hours, they were dressed and could not believe they were the same two persons. Rick stared in the mirror at what appeared to be his former self. Alec had a warm winter jacket, but Rick only had his windbreaker. They locked up their room and headed out the building. On the way out they stopped at the desk. Jimmy, the desk clerk looked up and asked, "Can I help you gentlemen?" They both laughed.

"You don't recognize Joe College?" Alec asked.

Jimmy stared in disbelief. "Believe me," he said, "the transition is amazing. You guys better lock your door tonight. I may not be able to resist coming in on you."

"Any other time, but not tonight," Alec countered. "We're on our honeymoon."

Jimmy flashed a wide, toothy grin. "Just one thing," he advised. "Get haircuts." Alec made a mental note to add that to his to do list.

The first thing on the list was a good brunch. Two doors up from the Y they spotted a neat little coffee shop. There they both had orange juice, eggs over, hash brown potatoes and coffee. It was the biggest meal Rick had eaten since he was kicked out of his house.

At the thrift store they bought some socks and underwear, six tee shirts, four pairs of jeans and a warm jacket for Rick. They were about the same size and intended to share. They went to a K-Mart and bought some lubricant, toiletries, and a cheap school knapsack for Rick. Happy with their purchases they spotted a barber shop on the way back to the Y and went in for a clipping. Not only did they get haircuts, they got buzz cuts. Neither of them liked the look and they laughed at each other.

Back in their room, they cut off all the labels from their new clothes, and distributed the clothing in the two knap sacks. They kept out the toiletries to use in the morning before checking out. Rick went over to Alec and embraced him. He cupped Alec's package in the palm of his hand.

"Before you push me away," Rick said, "I'm not the least bit hungry. That brunch is going to last me all day. Please, let's make love until dinner. Then we'll have a light bite and make love again until we fall asleep."

"That sounds like a great plan. You'll get no argument from me," Alec said. "I hate to remove these fresh smelling, clean clothes."

"You better get naked quick or I'll be forced to rip your clothes off!!!"

Rick was first to get into bed with Alec right on his ass, literally. They lay quietly in bed facing each other. At the exact same moment they wrapped their arms around each other. Their lips met in passion. Their tongues dueled. Their palms stroked the other's erect cock. Their bodies responded like well oiled machines. At just the right moment, Alec flipped around into a sixty-nine position and they began to lick up and down their shafts and across their heads. Their tongues tried to penetrate their piss slits to no avail. Rick tried desperately to stop himself, but when Alec's tongue brushed across his cock head, he came gushing out. He released Alec's cock and gave one primordial scream of pleasure. Alec forced his cock back into Rick's mouth and seconds later, he came also. His cock remained hard as did Rick's. Alec flipped around again and sought Rick's lips. They passed their juices back and forth between them.

They lay wrapped up in each other's arms, crunching their cocks together. Neither ever lost his initial hardon. After awhile Alec said in a dreamy voice, "Are you a top or a bottom?"

Rick laughed. "I don't know. I'm a virgin there," he informed Alec.

Alec laughed harder. "Me too, except for the rape, and that doesn't count," he said. "Let's try both ways. He grabbed the lube he had placed on the bed table, and squeezed some onto his fingers. He generously started to lubricate Rick's man hole and when he thought that Rick was as greased as he could get, he spread the lube all over his cock. Rick was on his back. Alec pulled Rick to the edge of the bed, and standing in front of him, he raised Rick's legs and positioned his cockhead at the opening to Rick's ass. He entered slowly with no trouble until he reached the sphincter. Tentatively, he pushed in. Rick was hurting, but he wasn't about to stop his lover.

"Keep going," Rick said, gritting his teeth. Alec's cock pushed past the sphincter. Rick gave an involuntary squeal and Alec stopped, but Rick urged him on, and before they both knew it, Alec was all the way in. They lay perfectly still. Little by little, Rick's pain diminished and he squeezed his ass muscles slightly. Alec was encouraged to start stroking. At first he did not move more than a couple of centimeters, but as passion grew so did the length of his strokes.

"This is the greatest," he informed Rick who was trying hard not to shit. As Alec increased the length of his strokes, Rick suddenly felt a strange sensation. Alec's cock was rubbing against something deep inside him that was making him feel like a million bucks. Something told him that he was about to orgasm again. He didn't want to because he wanted to fuck Alec next, but there was no stopping the inevitable. He came squealing with delight. His cum spurted up his body and squished between them. When he came, his ass hole constricted, putting Alec over the edge. Rick could feel each spurt filling his bowels. He counted at least five.

"That was wonderful," they both said in unison and broke out laughing.

"I love you," Rick said.

"I love you too," Alec whispered in Rick's ear.

"I want to fuck you now," Rick said, "but I'm all done out. "I need to recover from two orgasms in a row. Can we have that dinner you promised, and continue this scene afterwards?"

Alec didn't answer. He just kissed Rick harder as his cock slipped out of Rick's ass. They fell asleep hugging each other.

It was late afternoon when they went to the showers. They were alone and took great pleasure in washing each other's backs and privates. Once again they were reluctant to leave the luxury of a shower. They showered again after they made love that night and once again in the morning.

It was about 8 AM when they checked out. Jimmy was not at the desk so they asked the clerk to say goodbye for them. They went first to the coffee shop, but this morning they were satisfied with a cup of coffee and an order of toast. They shared the toast. Their splurge was over. It was time to conserve money. After breakfast they headed to the Greyhound Bus Terminal.

Alec got a schedule for a bus route that would take them as far as Jacksonville, Florida. He politely asked the ticket seller the prices for each stop from the first stop in Georgia to the last stop in Jacksonville. He went into a huddle with Rick and they decided that the most economical way to go was to ride the bus into southern Georgia and walk and hitchhike down to Key West. This way they would not only save money but they could check out Palm Beach, Ft. Lauderdale and Miami before heading for The Keys. Even though Alec's heart was set on Key West, there was always the possibility that another location in Florida might appeal to them more. At the moment the only thing that appealed to either of them was to be in a warm climate.

They sat in the terminal waiting to board the bus. Alec glanced down at his ticket and uttered, "Shit!"

"What?" Rick asked.

"Look at the date on the tickets. It's December 24th, Christmas Eve, I had no idea. Forgive me love. I would have bought you a present had I remembered."

Rick smiled. "Foolish jerk," he said. "You have given me the best Christmas present I ever got. You have given me yourself and a brand new life. Thanks Alec, for such a marvelous gift."

The bus left at 10 AM. The two young men were able to stow their knapsacks and Alec's guitar in the strapped overhead bin. They took seats towards the rear of the bus, first making sure that the seats reclined. They would have to sleep on the bus for two nights, and reclining seats were a priority for them.

Along the way to Key West. the two men encountered many adventures. Some events were mundane, but some were worth writing about. It would also be nice to know if they found success and happiness in Key West, but all that are tales for another time.

Tale Two: On The Bus

The big bus pulled out of the terminal and Rick and Alec sighed with relief. They reclined their seats and hoped to nap before the first stop for lunch on the long road to Georgia. The first hop of the journey was a mere two hours long. They would stop in Bangor for lunch and a pit stop. There was a small bathroom aboard, but it was nothing like the facilities of a roadside stop. Rick and Alec knew that Greyhound would choose the best places. At any rate, anything would be better than the Tent City, under the South Bridge, which had been home to Alec for many years and home to Rick for two months.

The entire trip from start to finish would be along Interstate 95. Alec wasn't sure how he knew this, but perhaps he had read it somewhere.

"South of Miami," he recited, "I 95 will merge into Route 1 and Route 1 goes all the way down to The Keys. It terminates in Key West at the southernmost point in the Continental USA." Rick didn't bother to answer. He was looking at Alec and smiling. He was constantly amazed that Alec knew so much. The last grade he had attended was the eighth. Nevertheless Alec was a fountain of information. Rick suspected that Alec might be the smartest man alive. With an education, who knows how far he could go.

Rick took Alec's hand and laid it on his thigh. Alec moved his palm up to Rick's crotch. They were at the back of the bus. There were only the bulkhead seats behind them and they were unoccupied. There was nobody to see them fondling each other.

Rick closed his eyes and tried to doze, but Alec was alert and he had eyed all the passengers as they entered the bus. He was sure the bus would fill as it went further south and stopped in big cities, but for now there were only six people besides themselves and the driver.

The first to enter was a woman in her late twenties. She had too much makeup on her face, and Alec had seen her eyeing Rick and him in the terminal. *She's a slut,* he thought, *maybe even a prostitute.* She took a seat in the center of the bus on the right side.

The second was a man in his seventies. He carried a paper bag which Alec suspected contained sandwiches and snacks. Alec chided himself for not thinking to do the same thing. He vowed to buy some snacks at the first stop. He concluded that the man was a widower, and he was going to visit one of his children, and probably grandchildren, for Christmas. Hence the happy grin, which never left his face. He took a seat about three rows back behind the driver.

The other four people were two couples who seemed to be travelling together. They were in their thirties, and Alec heard them say that they were getting off in Bangor. He figured that they were related and also going home for Christmas. They sat across the aisle from each other in the row behind the elderly man.

The bus driver was about fifty. He was portly and all business and efficiency, but he had a pleasant face. He smiled a lot and Alec loved the way his eyes crinkled when he grinned. Alec had to wonder why he was working on Christmas Eve, and he concluded that he was single and had no family. Alec suddenly felt sorry for him and determined to befriend him when they stopped for lunch. This being Christmas Eve, Alec figured that there would be very few new passengers the rest of this day and tomorrow. By the day after

Christmas they would be below New Jersey and probably the bus would fill up.

About a half hour into the trip, they were already on I-95. Alec was finished analyzing the other passengers. He was already bored and Rick had dozed off. He would have gone up front to sit behind the driver to strike up a conversation, but a big printed notice over the front windows prohibited him. DO NOT SPEAK TO DRIVER WHILE BUS IS IN MOTION it warned. Rick was seated at the window and Alec was on the aisle. He got up and took the window seat in front of Rick.

Alec was surprised to see that it was snowing. He hadn't seen a threat of it at breakfast. He became mesmerized by the swirling flakes. He glanced forward and could see the windshield wipers grinding hard to keep up with the wind tossed flakes. The driver didn't seem to be bothered at all. Alec closed his eyes, and tried to doze. He never fell asleep, but his eyes were closed for quite awhile. When he opened them the snow had stopped, but the sky was full of the kind of clouds that Alec recognized as "snow clouds." He returned to his seat. He took Rick's hand and laid it on his crotch. He wondered when they would make love again.

When the bus entered the rest stop in Bangor, the old man and the two couples removed some carry on bags, said goodbye to the driver and left the bus. The woman made no move to get up, but Rick and Alec did. The driver was standing at the door helping his passengers to negotiate the steep steps getting off the bus.

"Is it safe to leave my guitar on the bus, Tim?" Alec asked. He took a look at the driver's name tag, Timothy Sanders.

"Perfectly safe," Tim said. I'll lock the bus. We have an hour here. I'll come and get you when it's time to go."

"It would be nice," Alec added if you would have lunch with Rick and me. We are only going to share a sandwich."

"Tim looked shock. "My pleasure," he answered. "You go on ahead. I want to ask the lady if she's getting off the bus because I want to secure it. If she wants to stay on board, I'll lock her in."

The rest stop consisted of a small hotel and a restaurant. They needed to go through the hotel lobby to reach the restaurant. Rick paid no attention, but Alec was pleased to see that the old man and the two couples were met by loving family members.

They visited the restroom first, but hurried out to get to the restaurant before Tim got back. They told the restaurant hostess that there would be three of them, and she sat them at a table for four. Before she left she put three menus on the table.

It took a few moments for Tim to arrive. He looked totally perplexed. "Sorry guys," he said, "I'm kind of confused. When I approached that lady, she was sound asleep. I woke her up and when she looked around she bolted out of the bus. It was like she wasn't supposed to be there. Anyway I locked the bus, and I'm not sure we'll see her again. She didn't have any luggage stowed below. None of you passengers did."

The waiter came over and Tim ordered a tuna salad sandwich on rye with a cup of coffee. Alec ordered an egg salad sandwich with lettuce and tomato, and Rick ordered a cup of coffee.

"Excuse me a moment," Tim said. "I forgot something. He got up and spoke to the waiter and returned immediately.

"Do you mind if I ask you guys a personal question?" The two men raised their shoulders to indicate that he could. "Are you guys a couple?"

Alec laughed. "Is it that obvious?"

"I'm afraid so. There's a whole lot of love passing back and forth between you. Besides, my gaydar never lies."

"You're gay, then?" Rick asked.

"Yes, I am boys, and I've never been ashamed to admit it. Now tell me how you two met."

Rick related his story of how he was forcibly thrown out of his house, and Alec told him about his father's fatal accident. They told him how they both ended up living with other homeless souls underneath a bridge. Now they were trying to get away to a better life. There were tears in Tim's eyes.

"How about you?" Alec asked. "Why are you working on Christmas Eve?

"I'll give you the condensed version, men. I met my lover when we were both twenty and working in a department store.

We had thirty glorious years together. He died two months ago of stomach cancer. Neither of us has any family, and even though I have good friends, they have their own lives. I've been pretty lonely, and I volunteered to work tonight so that some family man could have his Christmas. We have a couple of short pit stops after lunch, but we'll stop for dinner in Manchester and after that when we stop in Boston, I'll be relieved by another driver."

Rick and Alec knew that they would have several drivers before reaching Georgia, but they would be sad to see Tim go. The waiter brought their food. He put down a cup of coffee and a full sandwich in front of each of them. Rick was about to say that he didn't order anything when Tim put his hand on Rick's arm. "Please," he said. "It's on me. Let's say it's a Christmas present."

Rick wanted to object, but he decided this kind gesture required him to be gracious. "Thank you," he said.

After lunch, they were walking back to the bus through the hotel lobby and stopped short. The lady from the bus had her arm through the arm of a much older man. They were waiting at the elevator.

"I guess she got what she was after," Alec whispered.

"I wish it was us going up to a hotel room," Rick murmured.

"It looks like it's going to be just the three of us on the bus, gents," Tim observed.

When they left the terminal to go outside, it was snowing rather hard. In fact visibility was very poor.

"This is not good," Tim said. He pulled out his cell phone and made a call to the state police. He identified himself and asked if it was safe to proceed. He listened intently and every once in awhile he said, "I see."

He turned to Rick and Alec. "The troopers have advised us not to leave. The snow is coming from the south and it's a real blizzard. In fact parts of I 95 are closed. Hold on a sec." He walked away so that Rick and Alec could not hear him, and he made another call. When he returned he had a huge grin on his face.

"It looks like you are going to get your wish Rick," he said. "I called Greyhound and when I told them the situation and said that

I only needed two rooms, they authorized me to charge our rooms to them." Rick and Alec looked at each other and grinned broadly. "If we are lucky, we'll be able to leave early tomorrow morning," Tim continued. "There isn't much to do around here to kill time until dinner."

"It's past check in time. If we can get the room now," Alec said, "I can think of lots to do."

"I'm jealous," Tim said. "Let's go to the desk and see what we can do.

"Wait," Alec said. "If they have a double room with two beds, or one king sized, I think we can agree on only charging Greyhound for one room."

Tim was stunned. "Are you sure?" he asked.

"Absolutely," they answered in unison. Tim put an arm around each young man and said, "Then let's go get a room, and let me thank God for the best Christmas gift I have ever received."

"We have to get our gear from the bus," Alec reminded everyone in his usual practical manner.

"Yes, I have an overnight bag on board also," Tim echoed.

They entered the room which had two queen size beds. Tim glanced into the bathroom. The shower is only big enough for one," he lamented. "Who wants to go first?" Nobody answered so Tim said, "I guess I will then." He started to undress so Alec and Rick did also. As soon as Tim was naked, he hesitated before heading to the showers. The wise man knew that Alec and Rick would want to check him out. Tim was overweight and a layer of fatty skin covered some of his cock. His manhood did not appear to be more than a little under average. But when he lifted the fatty skin, wow. His cock was revealed. It was much fatter than either of the two young lovers, and it was nearly six inches flaccid.

"You'll do nicely," Rick said. His mouth was watering. "Get yourself cleaned up, and don't stay in the shower forever. We're wasting time."

Seven or eight minutes later, Tim came out of the bathroom, drying himself. His staff was at half mast. Rick ran to the bathroom to shower next. Alec sat down on the edge of one of the beds and motioned to Tim. Tim came over to Alec who immediately consumed Tim's cock into his eager mouth. Instantly Tim was hard. After just a few short strokes of Alec's educated tongue, Tim pulled out.

"Please," he said. It's been so long. My partner and I didn't have sex for months during his illness and I haven't had sex since he died. I don't want to cum yet. I hope you boys will let me be the lucky guy in the middle."

Alec's infectious grin enveloped his face. "Tim, baby, this is your afternoon. Rick and I have a lifetime together." Tim leaned down and kissed Alec passionately on the lips. Just then Rick came out of the shower.

"Hey," he yelled, "don't start without me." Alec smiled and went into the bathroom.

"Alec said I could be in the middle. Is that alright with you?" Tim asked Rick.

"Tim, honey," Rick answered, "before this day and night are over, we'll each have a go at the middle position." He walked over to Tim and kissed him. Tim fell to his knees and took Rick's erect cock inside of his mouth. He stopped after a few strokes and said, "That's just a sample, sweetie."

When Alec came out of the shower, he took the lube out of his knapsack. He looked at Tim and said, "Rick and I are monogamous and don't use condoms. You are the first guy we have shared our bed with. Are you safe or do we need to dress and find a drug store in this hotel?"

Tim laughed. "I told you. My partner and I were monogamous also and I haven't been with anyone since he died. Going commando would be my preference."

With no hesitation, Rick lay down on his back and raised his legs. Alec lubricated his ass and then rubbed lube all over Tim's huge uncut cock. He helped Tim to enter Rick's waiting love canal, and when he was all the way in, Alec began to grease Tim's ass. "Gerry, my late partner, was bigger than anyone I ever saw," Tim informed them. "Unless I've shrunk, you won't need much of that stuff." Nevertheless, Alec greased Tim generously and then rubbed some lube on his very erect cock. As Tim had promised, Alec entered him too easily. He feared that there would not be enough friction to bring him to climax, but he needn't have worried. When Tim felt that Alec was in to the hilt, he constricted his ass and he was tight enough for Alec.

Alec started stroking first and then Tim picked up the rhythm. When Alec and Tim had established the metronome like rhythm, Rick began to rise up and down with them. Even though Tim was a little more than thirty years older than they, he was so love starved that he came first, followed shortly by Alec. Rick was close to cumming, but he didn't, so when Tim pulled out of him, he immediately went down on Rick and sucked him to climax.

They switched positions every so often. The first switch had Alec on his back, Rick in the middle and Tim on top. The third time around, Tim was done cumming for the day, and he took the bottom position with Alec in the middle and Rick on top. After the third round, they were all exhausted and fell asleep in one bed. Alec woke first and fortunately he was at the edge of the bed. Tim was in the middle and Rick was against the wall. He got out of bed and looked at his watch. It was 5 PM. Then he opened the curtain a little and looked out. It was still snowing, but it was not blowing so much.

He decided to shower again and dress for dinner. When he got out of the bathroom, he looked at his two companions and smiled. Tim was giving Rick a blow job, and Rick was fully hard and moaning softly. Alec decided not to interrupt, until he heard Rick scream out as he came yet again.

"Great job," Alec said to Tim, and he began to applaud. Rick and Tim turned red. You guys should shower again so we can go down for dinner.

They entered the hotel dining room at 6 PM. Tim told them that they should order a Christmas dinner because it was on him and they were not to object. It was his pleasure. They were not in a financial position to argue. Tim saw the prostitute at a dinner table with her john. Tim excused himself and went over to ask her if she would be reboarding the bus since her ticket was to Boston. She politely told him she would make other arrangements. Tim was secretly delighted. He and his two saviors would be alone on the bus, at least until Manchester.

The three of them ordered turkey with cranberry sauce and candied yams. It hadn't been that long ago that Rick had enjoyed such a meal but for Alec the memory was distant. As they were waiting for a dessert of apple pie ala mode, Tim called the highway patrol.

"Good news," he said. "The storm is moving north of us and the crews are clearing the highway. They expect to be reopened all the way south of here by 3 or 4 in the morning. What say, we get a wake up call about 4 AM and get going. We can have breakfast in Manchester, instead of dinner. Boston was not supposed to be a food stop, just a place to board and disembark passengers, and change drivers. You guys will have lunch there."

"I say, let's go for it," Rick said, and Alec nodded in agreement.

"Will you dine with us?" Alec asked Tim in mock fashion.

"Yes guys, I'll have breakfast in Manchester with you, but Boston is my home and I'll say goodbye to you there. I want you to know I'll never forget you and what you did for me. You have my gratitude forever." Tim took his card out of his wallet and gave it to Alec. "This is where you can reach me. When you get settled, I'd appreciate if you would write or call me and let me know how you guys are making out. I kind of wish I could be your father."

Both young men had tears in their eyes. Each of them took one of Tim's hands and squeezed it, knowing they would do more when they were back in their room. Unfortunately, Tim was all done out and declined any further sexual favors. However, he begged them to either fuck him or let him go down on them. Alec opted for a blow job, and while Tim was blowing him, Rick fucked Tim. Both of them had yet another fantastic orgasm.

They left at 5 AM and by midnight of the following day; they were on the New Jersey Turnpike near the Delaware border. The bus was now at least three quarters full. Earlier that day, in Red Bank, NJ two middle age men got on the bus and took the two seats across the aisle from Alec and Rick. They were very outgoing and introduced themselves immediately as Ken and John. They also let the guys know that they were going to Key West on a two week winter vacation.

"The only reason we are taking the bus," John said, "is that Wimpy here is afraid to fly."

"Where are you guys going?" Ken asked.

"We're going to Georgia to begin with. After that, we'll see. Just not sure," Rick said.

"Vagabonds are you?" Ken asked.

"Are you sitting way back here for the same reason we are?" John asked, arching his eyebrows. Alec and Rick did not feel like answering. These guys were beginning to annoy them. "We promise not to peek," John continued, and if we do, we promise not to tell." More silence from the other side of the aisle.

After the Red Bank stopover, the bus resumed its trek on the highway. The next stop was a couple of hours away in Dover, Delaware. As soon as the driver hit the highway, he shut the lights so that anyone who wanted to sleep could do so. Alec and Rick reclined their seats, put their shoulders together and closed their eyes. They actually fell asleep.

Alec, sitting on the aisle, was awakened by strange noises. They seemed to be coming from Ken and John. He glanced over at them. John was down on Ken greedily sucking his partner's cock. Ken's eyes were closed and he was making some weird noises, while John was making slurping noises.

Alec was instantly aroused and he poked Rick in the ribs. He put his hand on Rick's mouth to prevent him from making any noise. When Rick seemed to be aware of his surroundings, Alec whispered for him to look across the aisle. It was difficult for the two of them not to stare so they did. They were shocked to hear Ken ask, "Do you guys want to join us?"

Rick whispered in Alec's ear. "I'd rather wait for the next pit stop and do it in a bathroom stall."

"No thanks," Alec answered Ken. Do you mind if we watch?"

"Not at all." It was John who answered.

Ken felt compelled to offer an excuse. "After all, we're on vacation," he murmured.

Until Alec and Rick reached Georgia, they could not get rid of John and Ken. At every food stop, they sat down at their table and they even followed them into the rest rooms.

"Aren't you going to let us see what you've got?" they teased the boys. Alec and Rick did a good job of remaining stoic, and breathed a sigh of relief when they reached their last stop in Georgia.

The afternoon temperature was in the mid fifties. The two lovers could not believe that it could be so temperate in the winter. They asked someone at the pit stop if there was a YMCA in town. Unfortunately there was not, but they would find one in Jacksonville about fifty miles south of there.

The men thanked him and smiled at each other. "Well," Rick said, let's see how lucky we are at hitch hiking. They had kept clean shaven, and bathed, and had clean clothes. They were in fact beautiful, and they were to find out that hitch hiking would be a snap for them.

They went down to the highway, stuck out their thumbs and prayed for the best.

Tale Three: On The Road

Rick and Alec found a place about fifty feet short of an entrance ramp to I-95 South. They reasoned that anyone entering the highway would have their directional signals on, and more importantly, they would have room to stop to pick up passengers before merging onto the highway. They hoped to get a ride to Jacksonville quickly, so they would arrive before sundown. Alec intended to find the YMCA and a busy corner, where he could play his guitar and sing.

The first three cars passed them by without so much as a glance, but the young men were happy to see that they all had begun to slow down before entering the ramp even if they didn't use their directional signals. The spot they chose was perfect. The fourth car pulled over. A very handsome man in his early forties was behind the wheel. He had blond hair and beautiful blue eyes. His face was clean shaven and his chin was square. He rolled down the window and smiled at the boys.

"Wheah ya'll headed fer?" he asked with a thick southern drawl.

"Jacksonville," Alec answered, flashing back his own infectious smile.

"That's mah home and that's wheah ahm goin," the handsome man answered. "Whah don't ya throw your geah on the back seat, and one a ya come sit up front with me."

Rick chose the back seat and Alec chose to ride shotgun.

"Wheah ya'all from and whah in the world ah ya hitchhiking?" he wanted to know. Before they could answer, the driver said, "But wheah ah mah manners? Mah name is Reverend Harlan Bassett? What names do y'all two go bah?"

"I'm Alec," the front seat passenger said. "Rick's the young dude in the rear."

"Pleased to meet ya," Harlan said. "You boys don't happen to be Baptists?" he asked.

"I don't practice any religion," Alec answered, "but Rick here, he's a Methodist."

"Well, that's too bad Alec," Harlan said. "Lahf's pretty empty without Jesus in it." Alec wanted to get out of the car right then and there, fearing a high dose of homophobia, but he held his tongue. He wanted desperately to get to Jacksonville before dark.

After that they rode in relative silence. Alec actually started to doze, when suddenly he felt a hand on his crotch. The hand was caressing him sensually. "Oh, Rick," Alec murmured in his sleep, and he put his hand on top of the other one.

"Just as ah thought," Harlan said, "you two are a gay couple. That's nahce." Alec woke with a start. It was Harlan's hand on his cock. It felt nice, so he didn't stop him. He looked behind him and Rick was dozing also.

"You boys got a place to stay tonaht?" Harlan asked.

"We planned on the Y," Alec answered, pushing Harlan's hand further into him so he could feel his erection.

"Ah live alone and ah got plenty of room. Whah don't you boys stay with me tonaht?"

"Sounds good to me," Alec said. He reckoned he could do his singing in the morning during rush hour. He completely forgot that tomorrow was Sunday. The miles flew by and soon enough Alec realized that they were in Jacksonville. Harlan pulled into the driveway of a pleasant looking bungalow. He pushed the remote garage door opener on his visor, and drove into the garage.

"Don't get out 'til the door is closed," he instructed. As soon as the door was closed, he leaned over and kissed Alec with an open mouth and a full tongue. Alec and Rick went into the house with their knap sacks in tow.

"Y'all hungry?" Harlan asked, "Do y'all want to eat something now, or should we get raht down to business and eat laytah?" Rick and Alec had not had sex since their encounter with Tim over three days ago.

"I think we can eat later," Alec replied. Harlan's toothy grin almost blinded him.

"Come with me," he said. He led them to a bedroom with a standard size bed. Three men in that bed would be a challenge. They undressed quickly and the boys were shocked. Harlan had a very small uncut penis. It was hard as a rock and no more than two inches long.

Remembering their encounter with Tim, Rick asked, "Would you like to be in the middle?"

"Ah don't do anal," Harlan answered, screwing up his face. "Ah just do oral, if it's OK with you boys." It was.

For over two hours, they formed daisy chains on the bedroom floor, changing cocks often. They all tried not to cum, but nature had its way--- twice, for all three of them. Tight as it was, they all lay crunched together in the small bed, enjoying the after glow. "You boys sure made mah day," Harlan said.

Eventually they showered, and Rick and Alec shaved. While they were doing that, Harlan unfroze three TV dinners. As they were cleaning up, Harlan said, "Stay the naht, boys and go to church with me tomorrah. You would honah me if you do, but don't indicate that y'all know me." They didn't see how they could refuse, so they said yes.

They expected that Harlan would want them to sleep with him in his undersized bed, but they were shocked when he gave them a private guest room and bath. When they were nestled between the clean sheets, they began to make love.

"I feel cheated," Alec said. "I need you inside of me. He produced the tube of lube which he had smuggled into bed, and the two boys fucked each other twice before falling asleep. The last words Alec heard from Rick were, "I love you.

All Harlan made for breakfast was a cup of coffee. "Ah don't eat before ah preach," he explained. Harlan dropped the boys off two blocks from the church in an alley. They walked to the church and took seats in the last row. They put their knapsacks down beside them in case they wanted to make a hasty retreat. The service was strange to them, but they followed along. At last, Pastor Harlan stood to deliver his sermon.

Rick and Alec were shocked. As sweet as he was, his sermon was all fire, brimstone, and damnation to hell. He raved and ranted against the homosexuals and urged his congregants to drive them from good Christian society. The boys looked at each other in total disbelief, and ran out of the church.

With the help of some pedestrians, they found their way to another nearby church, also Baptist. When the service was over, Alec stood at the foot of the stairs, played his guitar and sang. The people leaving the church stood mesmerized. Alec had placed a baseball cap at his feet with a dollar bill in it. By the time he put his guitar away, they had collected $32.00 from the good people of this church and from some people passing by.

They were able to both hitch hike and walk back to the highway. Again they stood at a south bound entrance ramp and again they had no trouble hitching a ride. A young man about their age stopped for them. Again they threw their gear in the back and Rick took the back seat, while Alec sat up front.

The driver asked where they were going. "Eventually to Key West," Alec said, "but we'll be happy to go as far as you go."

The young man stuck out his hand. "I'm Marty," he said. I was home for Christmas, but I'm going back to school early so I can spend New Year's Eve with my buddy. I'll be ending up in Ft. Lauderdale if that suits you guys. We should get there about dinner time."

"It suits us fine," Alec said. I'm Alec and my partner is Rick." He said 'partner' on purpose. He wanted to gauge Marty's reaction. His gaydar was hard at work.

"You guys are a couple then," Marty noted. Alec nodded. Marty grinned.

"I thought so," he said, "or rather I hoped so. My partner and I live off campus in Ft. Lauderdale. If you guys need a place to stay tonight, we can give you a couple of sleeping bags."

Rick laughed. "We only use one bag when we sleep together," he said, thinking back to their first night together.

"That's entirely up to you," Marty said. "Maybe the four of us could have a little party." He leaned over and patted Alec's crotch. Alec smiled back at Marty. It was going to be another interesting, maybe wonderful, night. *Yes,* he thought, *we're a long way from tent city.*

Early in the evening Marty pulled into the parking lot of a six story apartment building. The three young men got out of the car. Marty retrieved a small suitcase from the trunk, and the boys grabbed their knapsacks. They took the elevator to the fourth floor and walked down the hall. Marty opened a door with his key and fell into the arms of a fairly short, but extremely good looking young man. They kissed passionately, with open mouths and dueling tongues.

When finally they separated, Marty introduced the boys to Tyler. They both held out their hands expecting a handshake, but Tyler hugged both of them in turn. He was obviously very huggy.

"Are you guys planning to stay on in Ft. Lauderdale for awhile?" Tyler asked.

"Maybe, for a bit," Alec said. "We'd really like to go on to Key West, but we don't mind a little layover here. It looks like a nice place."

"And warm!" Rick added.

"I hope you don't mind," Alec went on, "Marty invited us to crash here."

"Nah, we get visitors all the time. Just so long as you don't mind our bedroom noises, we're cool with it. Just buy your own food," Tyler said. He turned to Marty. "Right now, we are going to test your hearing. I haven't seen Marty in a week, and I'm dragging him into the bedroom, where we are going to make some noise." He went to a hall closet and pulled out two sleeping bags.

"You guys can use these. The bathroom is over there," he pointed, "but if you want to eat, there's a nice little restaurant down at the corner."

"It's a little early," Rick said. "Will you guys want to be eating later? We can wait for you."

Marty and Tyler looked at each other. "Yeah," Marty said, "wait for us." They disappeared into the bedroom closing the door behind them. Alec and Rick spread the two sleeping bags on the living room floor. They stripped quickly and Alec got the lube from his knapsack. They were both fully erect. Before they had a chance to lie down, the door to the bedroom opened and a naked Tyler emerged.

"Sorry guys," he said, "I need a fresh tube of lube from the bathroom." Of course he checked Alec and Rick out and whistled. "You two guys sure are well hung. Hey Marty, check this out. I think we should all play together. What do you two guys say?"

"I have no objection," Alec said. He looked at Rick who nodded in approval.

"I've got an idea," Marty said. Tyler and I have been apart for almost a week, and I want to be with him. Why don't we enjoy our own partners now, and then go out for a bite to eat. When we get back, we can form a rotating daisy chain, and then for the grand finale, we can switch partners. They all thought that was a great idea. Before they went back to the bedroom, Tyler asked Rick and Alec if they needed anything. They both shook their heads, and fell to the floor.

They couldn't have known it, and they certainly didn't compare notes, but both couples did the exact same thing. They warmed up with a lusty game of sixty-nine. Then Tyler fucked Marty and Alec fucked Rick. The two bottoms came before their partner's exploded in their asses. Rick, as usual, screamed when he came, and both Marty and Tyler made gasping noises, which Rick and Alec clearly heard. The four of them headed to the bathroom to clean up at the exact same time. They laughed when they saw each other. Marty and Tyler decided to be good hosts, and they let their guests go first. There certainly wasn't room for four in the tiny bathroom.

The little restaurant was perfect for Alec and Rick. They served a complete meal from appetizer to a beverage and dessert, all for a very nominal amount.

"I hope the floor wasn't too uncomfortable," Tyler remarked as they began to eat.

"It was fine. Besides we were too busy to notice," Rick answered. They all laughed. After that they exchanged stories of how they all met. Tyler and Marty were assigned to be lab partners in freshman chemistry.

"I kept brushing up against him until he finally got the hint," Marty said. Tyler smiled at him and squeezed his hand.

When they heard Rick and Alec's story they were all sympathy, but Alec said, "Don't cry for us. All's well that ends well."

Neither Marty nor Tyler were as well hung as Rick and Alec, but very few are. Nonetheless they were very ample. Tyler was not cut, but Marty was. They played in a daisy chain for nearly an hour until they realized that they couldn't hold out much longer.

"I've got an idea," Marty said. Alec isn't cut and neither is Tyler. I'll take Alec because I am very adept at handling foreskin, and I am sure Rick is too. So Rick you take Tyler."

"It doesn't matter to me," Rick said, "but who gets the bed?" Tyler and Marty flipped a coin and Marty won.

In the morning, Marty and Alec awoke wrapped up together, and Rick and Tyler woke up the same way. One at a time they attended to their bathroom needs and Tyler made juice, coffee and toast for breakfast. As they sat around talking, Marty said, "Look guys, we're a couple of days shy of New Year's Eve. I know you said you want to go on to Key West, but why not stay with us for a few days more and spend the holiday with us. We had planned to spend a quiet night at home entertaining ourselves, but now the entertainment possibilities are endless? What do you say?"

"I say it sounds good," Alec replied.

"Yes, it sounds like a plan to me," Rick echoed.

Marty and Tyler spent the day showing Rick and Alec around gay Ft. Lauderdale. Alec took his guitar and baseball cap with him, and when they were at a very busy corner, he set up shop. The other three guys had no problem listening to him. He had the kind of voice and charisma that people paid to hear, and they were getting a free concert. He played for about an hour and a half and made $57.00.

During their escorted tour, Rick noticed that almost every gay bar and restaurant had signs indicating that waiters were wanted. One of them had an additional sign. "Entertainers see Ryan." Rick pointed the sign out to Alec and they smiled at each other.

"Would you excuse us, please," Alec said to Tyler and Marty. We'll be right out."

"Sure," Tyler said, "We'll have a drink at the bar while we're waiting."

Alec found Ryan, while Rick found the day manager. When the day manager checked Rick's package out through his tight jeans, he was hired on the spot. He didn't even ask Rick if he had experience. Actually, he did. Rick had worked as a waiter in a malt shop all during his junior year and in his senior year for as long as he had lived at home.

"We wear khaki shorts and white tee shirts for waiting tables, and make sure the shorts are good and tight. Is that a problem for you?" the day manager asked.

"No problem at all," Rick answered. "When do I start?"

"You can work lunch tomorrow. Be here at 11. If you want to, and if I like your work, you can do dinner also," the day manger, Dave, answered. And you have to work New Year's Eve also. On most days you'll be free by 10, but it will be all night on New Year's Eve. They shook hands, and Rick joined Tyler and Marty at the bar with his thumb up in the air.

"Our entertainment schedule is booked solid," Ryan told Alec, "but I need a piano or a guitar to play and sing during dinner. The regular entertainers start at about 10 and work until 2 AM. You don't get paid. It's strictly on tips." Ryan looked at Alec's case. "Guitar?" he asked.

"Yes, I play guitar and sing," Alec answered.

"Go ahead. Show me," Ryan sounded bored.

Alec started to sing, and Ryan's jaw dropped down. "Damn, you're good." He interrupted Alec after just a few notes. "You're hired. Can you start tomorrow?"

"You bet," Alec said.

"Be here about 4:30 PM, and you better have plenty of numbers. Also if you had plans for New Year's Eve, remember, you have to work then also." Ryan stood up and shook Alec's hand.

Alec joined the other guys at the bar. "I'm employed," he said, "but New Year's Eve is out."

"I know," Marty said. "Rick just told us, so we made reservations here for dinner on New Year's Eve, and whatever comes afterward. We want to share the night with you. You're starting a new life in a new year."

"That's great of you guys," Alec said. "but we have one more thing to take care of. You are better friends than we had ever hoped to have, but Rick and I can't stay with you forever. We need to find a place of our own."

"I think I know just what will fit your needs, at least until you get on your feet," Tyler said. "There's a furnished, efficiency apartment for rent in our building. They want $350 a month and probably a security deposit. Can you guys swing that?"

"No," Rick said.

"Yes," Alec said.

Rick looked at Alec in amazement. Obviously he had squirreled away more than Rick knew about. "We can swing it," Alec reinforced his statement.

Tyler stood up quickly and said, "Hell men, let's go look at it."

After tent city, the efficiency apartment looked like an estate in heaven to Rick and Alec. It had a bathroom with a stall shower, and consisted of one big room. There was an alcove at one end of the room with a sink, a small refrigerator, and a two burner stove. Two cabinets hung above them. The rest of the room contained a tiny kitchen table, two chairs, a clothes closet, sleep sofa, a side table, and a dresser. The cabinet contained dishes and kitchen utensils, and the top shelf of the clothes closet contained linens and pillows for the sleep sofa. There was a common laundry room at the end of the hall. They would need to use quarters for the washer and dryer.

They told the landlord that they didn't know how long they would be in town and so they couldn't sign a lease. He was satisfied that they take a month to month tenancy, but he wanted first and last month's rent, and a like amount for a security deposit. Rick looked at Alec forlornly, but Alec said to the landlord, "It's a deal."

Alec paid the landlord and got a receipt. He made sure the receipt indicated what the $1,050 was for. If nothing else, Alec was street wise. Rick was very naïve in the ways of the world.

"You can move right in," the landlord said. "What's left of December is free."

Yes, Rick intended to have a long talk with Alec about their finances.

"We better make a lot of money," Alec told Rick. We are almost out of our bankroll. That answered Rick's question. No further talk would be necessary.

The apartment was two doors down from their new friends. Alec told them that he would like to spend their first evening alone in their first apartment. Tyler and Marty fully understood, but asked if they could afford to go out to dinner to celebrate their good fortune. Rick looked at Alec, who smiled and nodded his head. "I'll have to ply my trade on street corners in the morning," he laughed. "There's nothing like a working girl on a street corner."

After dinner, when Alec tried to put his key into the door of their new apartment, he was shaking, and he had to steady his right hand with his left. The two young men were giddy with excitement. Less than a week ago they had been homeless, living in a fabricated shelter in a tent city, and here they were entering their first apartment as a couple.

They opened the sofa bed, put on the linens, and covered the pillows with cases. They made love that night like it was their first time, and like there would be no tomorrow. They caressed each other's cocks with their tongues in a sensuous, long lasting game of sixty-nine. When they recovered, they fucked each other, not once, but three times. It was a night to remember. They did not fall asleep until 3AM.

Still, Alec was up early, and he woke Rick.

"I'm off to try to make a few bucks," he said. "First we'll have breakfast at that place on the corner." He handed Rick a twenty dollar bill. "We're almost at the bottom of the barrel. After breakfast I'll go to work, and you go buy some food staples for the apartment. I'll meet you back here at ten o'clock. I know you have to be at work at 11. I'm glad we bought khaki shorts, but you may need more. First chance we get we'll go to a thrift shop."

"Now that we have an address," Rick added, "we should get state ID's as soon as possible. I'm sure they will want something at work for starters."

"Yes," Alec agreed. "We'll take care of it first thing in the morning on the day after New Year's Day.

While Rick shopped, Alec made $21.00 at a busy pedestrian corner in just a half hour. He recited a silent prayer that the tips at the restaurant would be as good or better. He could not imagine at this point, just how popular he would be.

One of the things Rick bought while he was out shopping was a sewing kit. As soon as he got home, he took his Khaki shorts and sewed new seams on the inside thighs. The shorts were as tight as he could make them, and still permit him to fit into them. His package was bulging, and he too had no idea how large his tips would be because of it. The old malt shop he had worked in was not a gay bar and restaurant. His package had held no meaning there.

As Rick admired his bulging shorts, he suddenly felt a chill and he shuddered. He felt a presence in the room and he instinctively looked in the mirror hanging over the dresser. A young man, bulging with muscles, stood behind him smiling. The apparition looked very much like Alec.

In that instant Rick knew that he and Alec had a guardian angel looking over them, and that angel was Alec's dad.

Tale Four: Under The Palm Trees

Rick and Alec had one night to practice their trades before the hustle and bustle of New Year's Eve. It was December 30th and the restaurant was relatively quiet. The regular patrons were saving their money and energy for the next night.

Rick arrived early. He filled out some employment information; address and social security number. Marty and Tyler had given their new friends, and fuck buddies, permission to use their telephone number until they could afford to get a land phone or cell phones.

Rick waited on the lunch crowd, and the day manager was more than pleased. He told him to stay for the dinner hour, and he could eat his own dinner before the customers arrived.

Alec arrived at 4:30, filled out some employment papers also, and ate dinner with the staff. After that he set up his props, a single chair, and a large bowl for tips. He placed a dollar bill in the bowl, and sat down on the chair. He started to play the guitar for a while before he began to sing. He played all during the dinner hour, while Rick was one of several waiters keeping the customers pleased with the food, drinks and especially the service. Every time Alec started to take a short break, the diners begged him to keep singing.

The club hired one entertainer to perform each night. The customers knew that if they wanted to hear a piano player, they could come around on Monday. If they wanted to see a comedian, then Tuesday was their night. Karaoke was Sunday night and so on. The entertainer that night was a well known local drag queen, who called herself Miss Fantasy. She came in around 9:30 in full drag costume, and when Alec had finished a set, she said to him, "Hey man, you are gorgeous. You're voice is something else. Thanks for warming up this light crowd for me."

"My pleasure," Alec responded. She kissed Alec on the top of his crew cut head.

By 10 PM the dining room was closed, and the lounge was beginning to fill. Miss Fantasy was lip syncing and moving among the crowd. Alec and Rick got ready to go home. The waiters did their own bussing, so Rick did not have to split his tips. Both their pockets were bulging with dollar bills, and this did not count the tips Rick had been given on credit cards. That would come with his first pay check, and it was an even greater amount than the cash tips he had received that night. Besides the cash, both men had been offered huge sums of money by older patrons to come home and spend the night with them. They diplomatically declined, but flirted enough to make the customers smile and want to return.

In their apartment, they flattened out the paper money and placed them in denomination order. They were shocked to find some fives among the singles. All in all between the two of them, they had $127.00.

"And this was a light night," Alec reminded Rick. Can you imagine what New Year's Eve should be like? We'd better open a bank account. We can't keep toting around all our earnings." They showered and went to bed too exhausted for anything else.

"I'll get you in the morning," Rick promised Alec. "But don't knock me out. I'm working lunch, and tomorrow we're serving dinners until 3 AM and closing at 4. I'll need all my strength."

"I'm only working my regular hours, so I'll go easy on you," Alec pledged. "I'm joining Marty and Tyler after my gig, and I'll wait for you."

They wrapped themselves up in each other's arms, fondled their partner's cock, and fell asleep that way.

Marty and Tyler did not come to dinner until 10 PM on New Year's Eve. They requested to be seated at a table in Rick's station. When Alec finished his gig, he joined them. The table was beautifully decorated with confetti and noise makers. When a staff member finished his shift, the management allowed them one free drink. Rick took their drink orders and told them that Marty and Tyler's first drinks were on him. When they objected, he winked at them. He also let them know that they had booked the last table turnover for the night, and after dinner they could stay at their table to celebrate the coming of the New Year or they could go to the lounge.

"I think we'll stay here," Tyler said. "You're part of our celebration, Rick."

When the huge crowd began to count down the seconds until midnight, Rick stood by their table. He grabbed Alec and they began to kiss passionately. "I am so lucky," he whispered to Alec, "I have everything I want now."

When Tyler and Marty were finished kissing each other, the four men kissed each other and embraced in a group hug.

"Don't go home tonight," Marty begged. "Sleep in our apartment." They all hugged tighter, which meant a resounding YES.

Alec thought, *I have a loving partner, good friends, a roof over my head, and a job. What more could a guy ask for?*

They got home that night exhausted, but too excited for sleep. It was decided that Alec and Tyler would sleep together that night, and Marty and Rick would make a pair, since it had been the opposite way the first time the four had made love together. Each of the two couples got each other off in a hot game of sixty nine, and then Marty suggested that they could all four fuck each other, but with two guys in the middle. Obviously one of them would be left out, but that could be remedied later.

Rick drew the short straw. He lay down on his back with his ass at the edge of the bed. Tyler then greased himself up good and entered him. Alec then entered Tyler, and Marty entered Alec. None of them moved for a time as they got used to each other. Marty was the first to move, stroking slowly at first and then a little faster. The others picked up the pace and soon all four were stroking to the same rhythm, with Rick thrusting instead of stroking.

One after the other they came. Rick's prostate was in overdrive, but somehow he managed not to cum, using sheer will power. When at last they separated, Rick put Marty on his back on the bed, and he entered Marty. He had not cum before but he was aching to do so. With Tyler and Alec cheering him on, he came screaming, and gushed up Marty's ass. Marty moaned in pleasure. They lay still for quite awhile before separating. They were now more than satisfied. Each one had cum orally, and each one had cum anally, and each one had enjoyed a cock in his mouth and up his ass. They couldn't think of a better way to celebrate a New Year, and a new life for Alec and Rick.

Alec and Rick returned to their own apartment to shower and sleep, but they all agreed to meet back at Tyler and Marty's for brunch the next day.

At about 11 AM the following morning, Alec and Rick were still asleep when they were awakened by loud knocking on their door. Rick jumped out of bed. "Who is it?" he croaked.

"It's Tyler. Alec has a call from Ryan at The Golden Cockerel," He called through the door, trying not to make too much noise. Alec jumped up. He was shaking and all he could think about was that he was being fired. Without realizing that he was naked, he ran down the hall and grabbed the phone in his friends' living room. Marty was still asleep in the bedroom.

"Alec," Ryan said. "I've got a dilemma. The singer for tonight just called and said that he was fed up singing down here and getting nowhere. He's going back to New York. As you know, we're closed today for lunch, but we are opening for dinner. Do you think you could do dinner and then sing in the lounge after that? Would it be too much for you? The gig in the lounge is $150.00 a night plus whatever tips you make."

"I'm your man," Alec beamed. "I'll see you later, and thanks Ryan."

Alec grabbed Tyler and kissed him. Alec forgot he was naked and Tyler did what comes instinctively. He grabbed Alec's cock and started stroking it. Alec got hard immediately and Tyler fell to his knees. He took Alec into him, and it wasn't long before Alec gushed several streamers down his throat.

"Wow," Alec said. "Thanks for the wake up call."

"Don't mention it," Tyler said. "What are we celebrating?"

"It looks like I'll be playing the lounge on Friday night's."

That night Alec went right from the restaurant to the lounge. Rick said he would have his one free drink, and meet him at home when he was done. Alec played from 10 PM until 2 AM, taking a ten minute break every twenty minutes. On one of his breaks, he was approached by a middle aged man who looked like he was right out of GQ. He really stood out in a crowd of scantily dressed twentyish year olds.

"Hi," the man said. "My name is Curtis James. You have an incredible voice. I work for the Fox affiliate out of Miami. Every year we hold auditions for American Idol. If you are the winner, you can audition first for the show, and not have to wait it out with thousands of others."

Alec had no idea what the man was talking about. "What's American Idol?" he asked in all innocence. Curtis looked at him in astonishment.

"You really don't know?" he asked. Alec was not about to relate to him the circumstances under which he had lived since he was fourteen, and the fact that he hadn't seen a TV show since the night he had been brutally raped by his foster father. Alec just shook his head.

"Well, my handsome young stud," Curtis said, "It's a national singing competition. The winner not only gets a recording contract, but more money than you ever dreamed of. The top ten also tour the country after the competition. Some of the non winners have hit it big also, after having been exposed to the country. Look, here's my

card." Curtis reached into his wallet and handed Alec his card. "The
local competition is on March 1. The regular auditions begin in the
summer. The judges are doing Miami in July. Come to my office on
March 1, and I'll personally escort you into the competition studio."

Six homeless years on the streets had made Alec very
suspicious. He was just waiting for the man to come on to him in
return for offering him this opportunity, but it never happened. Instead
the man said, "Let's not talk so much, young man. I just want to hear
you sing." Alec stuffed the card into his pocket, and went back to
work. By the time he got home that night, he had forgotten all about
the card Curtis had given him.

He found Rick fast asleep on top of the covers. He was lying
on his back and his limp dick hung down invitingly over his balls.
Alec shut the light and got undressed in the near darkness. The room
was romantically lit by moonlight. Instead of getting into bed on his
side, he stood over Rick, leaned down and took Rick's cock into his
mouth. Rick moaned and stirred, but he didn't awaken immediately.
After a short time, Alec could tell from Rick's moans, and the way his
ass had begun to squirm, that he was awake and fully enjoying Alec's
little present. With his usual scream, Rick squirted copiously into
Alec's waiting receptacle.

Alec refrained from swallowing. Instead he kissed Rick with
open lips and the two lovers shared Rick's juices together. Finally
Alec climbed into bed. The two men embraced and fell fast asleep.

They both worked six days a week. Sunday was a day off
for each of them. There was no formal entertainment on that day.
The restaurant and the lounge both featured karaoke all evening.
The Sunday waiters and some of the bartenders were mostly college
students who worked part time on Sundays and filled in for ailing
regulars when needed. There were a few Sunday mornings when
Rick had suggested attending a gay church he had heard about. Rick
had been given a very strict religious upbringing. Alec would have
none of it. "Nonsense," he called it. He asserted that if God really
existed, he would not have taken his father and left him so destitute
at such a young age. Instead Sunday mornings were spent cleaning
house and doing laundry.

Before putting any clothes in the wash machine, Rick always checked the pockets. He emptied the trousers Alec had worn Friday evening at his gig. He found a few used tissues and a business card. He threw away the tissues and pocketed the business card. He intended to ask Alec what he was doing with the business card of a Fox executive. But now it was his turn to forget about it.

Back in the apartment, Alec was finishing up the house cleaning. They never folded the sofa bed anymore unless they were expecting company. It seems that they were constantly hopping into bed to play. After the laundry and the housework were done, they planned on having brunch out. While the wash machine was churning, they had time for a little horse play. They never passed up an opportunity.

Later on, while they were having Sunday brunch, Rick remembered the card and asked Alec about it. When Alec told him what it was all about, Rick got really excited. He was very familiar with American Idol and he immediately said, "Alec this is a once in a lifetime opportunity. You have to do it. If you don't want to do it for yourself, then do it for us."

The current season of American Idol was half completed. Rick had purchased a Sunday paper and he searched the TV listings for American Idol. They would both be working during the next show, but Marty and Tyler had a TV set and a VCR and Rick intended to ask them to tape the show so Alec could see what it was all about. The show aired Wednesday evening and results were broadcast on Thursday evening. When Rick told Tyler and Marty why he wanted them to tape the show, they became more excited than Rick. Only Alec remained mistrusting, disbelieving and very blasé.

Tyler and Marty were in school all day Wednesday, but when Rick and Alec got home a little after 10 PM, they all got comfortable in front of the TV set, and Marty inserted the tape into the VCR. After each of the remaining seven contestants had completed their singing, and been mostly bashed by the judges, one or the other of them would say, "Alec, you're much better than that."

When the tape was over, Rick hugged Alec and pleaded, "Do it baby. You have a real shot at it."

"We'll see," Alec answered without much conviction. He kept thinking that life had been pretty cruel to him, and he had no reason to believe he would even make the show. Still, ever since he had met Rick, his fortunes had dramatically improved. Suddenly, he gasped. He distinctly heard a voice whisper in his ear. *Do it Alec.* It was his father's voice. He would know that voice anywhere. Rick had told him that he had seen a man in their apartment and that it was Alec's father. Alec had scoffed at him and told him to stop drinking.

"What's wrong?" Rick asked him.

"Nothing baby," he answered. "I just decided that I'll audition. What have I got to lose?"

On July 7th, Alec entered the posh hotel in downtown Miami. His guitar hung from its strap over his shoulder. He had a folder full of credentials, and when he presented them at a check in desk, he was awarded a name tag and the number 12. The pretty girl at the table directed him to a large auditorium. He was to be the twelfth audition among all the other regional winners. He panicked when he saw so many people in the room and the thousands more waiting outside.

I'm crazy, he thought. *What the fuck am I doing here?*

He was about to bolt out of the room, when a young man stuck his hand out at him and said, "Hey man, how yer doin'? I'm Andy from Delaware." He shook Alec's hand vigorously, and Alec realized he had no visible means of escape. "I won my regional in Philadelphia," Andy continued. "Where are you from?"

Alec's stomach was in knots. He wanted so much to bolt out of there, but he got himself together and sat down next to Andy. "I'm Alec from Ft. Lauderdale, Florida."

"Pleased to meet ya Alec. I'm wishin' you the best of luck. Wouldn't it be great if we both went on to Hollywood?"

"Yeah sure," Alec grumbled. He noted that Andy's number was 11, and he reasoned that Andy would be so good the judges wouldn't even consider him. Alec went into a deep funk and withdrew into himself. Suddenly he could hear Rick in the back of his mind, admonishing him to stay positive. Good old Rick had given him a pep talk before he took the Tri Rail to Miami.

I wish I could stay positive, he thought. Then he heard another voice. This one did not come from the back of his head. This one spoke directly into his ear. "Stop fretting, boy. You're a winner." It was definitely his dad. Alec gave out an involuntary sob.

"What's wrong?" Andy asked. "Do you need help?"

Alec brightened. "No," he said. "I'm fine and dandy. What the hell! We have nothing to lose. Let's relax, have fun, and enjoy the moment." The two young men gave each other a high five.

"Hey Alec," Andy said. "Where are you staying tonight? I've got reservations in a small motel near the airport. My plane leaves tomorrow afternoon, win or lose."

Without thinking, Alec answered. "I'm going home after the audition. If you want to save the motel costs, I can give you a sleeping bag and you can stay with me."

Andy's eyes lit up. "That would be great," he said. Then he hesitated, before he said, "Can I tell you something?"

"Sure."

"I have no motel room. I hitched rides down here and I'll be going back the same way. My family supports me emotionally, but they don't have a pot to pee in to help me out financially. I'm sorry I lied," he added. Poor Andy looked so sad.

"It's OK man," Alec soothed him. "I was homeless and hitched down to Florida from Maine in the winter. I know what it's like to be broke. I was out on the streets from the time I was fourteen until recently." Andy looked like he might cry so Alec put his arm around him and was shocked when Andy put his head on Alec's shoulder. It was an awkward moment so Alec disengaged himself and pulled out his cell phone. He and Rick had invested in cell phone service after earning their first week's bounty of wages and tips.

He dialed Rick who answered on the first ring. "Relax buddy," Alec said. I haven't auditioned yet. Would you please borrow a sleeping bag from Marty and Tyler? I'm bringing home an overnight guest."

"Is he cute?" Rick asked jokingly.

"Adorable... No I won't call you after the audition. You'll have to wait and see."

Hours later, Rick paced up and down. Alec had not called and it was dinner time. He should be home by now. Rick was certain that Alec had failed to make the cut and was reluctant to come home. Suddenly the phone rang. It was Alec.

"We're on the train," he said, "I'll tell you all about it when I get home." Rick was relieved, but it bothered him that he could not read yes or no in Alec's tone.

On the train Alec decided to tell Andy about his living arrangements, lest he be shocked later, run out, and have no place to go.

"Andy, I gotta tell you something," Alec began. "I'm gay and I have a partner. We sleep nude. You are still welcome to sleep over in a sleeping bag, but if that grosses you out, you can get off the train in Ft Lauderdale. At least you'll be forty miles closer to home, that is, if you are still heading north."

"No problem, Alec," Andy responded. "I've often wondered what and how you gay guys get yourself off. Can I watch?"

Alec was stunned, and he felt a jolt in his groin. "I think it would be a turn on for me, but I'd have to leave it up to Rick."

"Fair enough," Andy responded. They sat in silence the rest of the trip.

When they entered the apartment, Alec took Andy's knapsack and put it in the closet. The little kitchen table was set for three, and a bridge chair was squeezed in at the table. Alec introduced Andy to Rick, who remembering Tyler's first greeting, hugged Andy instead of shaking his hand.

"Watch it stud," Alec said. "Andy's straight."

"Oops, sorry," Rick muttered.

"No need to be sorry. You didn't do anything wrong or make me feel uncomfortable," Andy said, and he gave Rick another hug.

"Enough bullshit," Rick suddenly yelled. "What the hell happened? Tell me before I bust."

"Sit down," Alec ordered. "I'm afraid I have bad news." Rick's jaw dropped. Alec continued. "You will have to be alone for however long it takes me to be eliminated from the competition, and if I make the top ten, you'll have to be alone while I'm on tour. Are you badly upset?" he asked and broke out laughing.

Rick jumped up and started to kiss Alec passionately with an open mouth. The two of them erected immediately and ground their cocks together. Then Rick remembered Andy, who was smiling at them and had his hand on his heart. "So sorry," Rick said.

"Never be sorry to have someone to love. There's not enough love in this world," Andy said. He buried his head in his hands and started to cry. Rick and Alec immediately embraced him. His shoulders were heaving, and when finally he calmed down, Rick said, "I made a beef stew guys. How about it?"

Andy and Alec went separately to the bath room to wash up. Later at dinner, Rick could see that Andy was trying to slow down, but he was eating like he hadn't eaten in weeks. Alec caught Rick's eyes and thoughts. He nodded and Rick knew that he was right.

They were just cleaning up, when there was a knock at the door. Marty and Tyler burst in and were surprised to see a third party in the room. They quickly recovered and demanded to know what had happened. Fearing that Alec would toy with them, Rick yelled out, "He's going to Hollywood." Are you guys going to make sure I won't get blue balls while he's gone?" They all laughed except Andy. He was unused to such talk, and he blushed a deep crimson.

After Tyler and Marty were introduced to Andy, Rick said, "Oh my God, Andy, I am so sorry. I never asked about you."

Andy smiled broadly. "I'm going to Hollywood with Alec. We asked, and we can room together. Isn't that great?"

"Do you guys want to join us at your place of employment tonight?" Tyler asked.

"No we took the day off and we'd better leave it that way," Alec said. "It's been a rough day and we just all want to relax. Besides I've got lots to talk to Andy about. You guys go on and we'll catch you tomorrow."

"OK, but don't the three of you start playing without us," Tyler quipped.

"Andy's straight so mind your tongues. In fact keep them in your mouths," Alec quipped. Tyler looked embarrassed and Marty hit him on the shoulder.

After they left, the three men sat down at the table. They sensed that Alec wanted to talk. He did, but he seemed to be addressing Rick.

"Rick honey," he began (Andy raised his eyebrows. He wasn't used to one man calling another, honey.) "Andy is broke, and he would have to hitch hike home. If he's willing, and doesn't mind sleeping on the floor in a sleeping bag, I'd like to ask him to stay with us until we leave for Hollywood." Before Rick could answer, Alec continued, this time addressing Andy.

"Andy, I'm pretty sure we can get you a job where we work. Have you ever waited on tables?"

"Many times," came the answer.

"Would you mind if it was in a gay bar? You're a hunk, and are apt to be hit on. Would that bother you?"

"I don't know," Andy answered. "It has never happened to me."

"So what's your answer?" Alec asked. Andy looked at Rick, who nodded and smiled. Rick's only thought was that now he and Alec had a chance to pay it forward for the kindness shown them by Tyler and Marty.

Andy nodded with tears in his eyes. "I swear I'll pay you for my room and board as soon as I can,"

"I know you will, Andy," Alec said. "Now we have one more hurdle." He looked at Rick. "I told Andy that we sleep nude and that since we live in one room, he will have to put up with us making love whenever the mood strikes us." Rick looked stunned. "Furthermore," Alec continued, "he said he'd like to watch. It would be a turn on for me. How about you?"

"Jerk," Rick said. "You should know by now that whatever turns you on, turns me on. Are you really Ok with this Andy?"

"Damn straight," Andy said. Then realizing how that came out, he laughed and said, "Oops." Everyone laughed.

"I've got one more confession," Andy said, looking at Alec. "I told you that I am straight, and I'm sure I am, but I'm a virgin.

I have never slept with a woman either. I only know I'm straight because of the way I feel about girls, and when I jack off I fantasize about the opposite sex."

"That's Ok with me," Alec said. "I am not bigoted against straights." Once again they all laughed.

"All this talk about sex has made me hot," Rick said. "I'm going to the bathroom first and getting ready for bed." In a flash, he disappeared into the bathroom while Andy and Alec got the sleeping bag ready.

"Please. Let's put it on your side of the bed," Andy requested. "It seems right seeing as how we are going to be room mates."

Moments later Rick came out of the bathroom. He was naked and fully erect. It was only natural for Andy to check him out and say, "Wow."

As Rick sat down on the bed on top of the covers, he said, "Save your wows. Wait until you see Alec." In a short time Alec joined Rick on the bed.

"You don't have to sleep nude like us," Alec said. "Do whatever you are comfortable with."

Andy went into the bathroom. He took much longer than Rick and Alec because he treated his body to a very long shower. He hadn't done more than wash himself in rest stops for several days. When he came out of the bathroom he was naked, but unlike Rick and Alec, he was flaccid.

"You're a wow yourself," Rick said. He turned off the bedside lamp. The room was not plunged into darkness. Moonlight bathed the small apartment.

"Are you sure I can watch?" Andy asked.

"Absolutely," they both answered.

Rick threw himself on top of Alec and they began a duel of tongues. They ground their cocks together and twisted and moaned. They couldn't see, of course, but Andy was beginning to get hard. He was shocked at what was happening to him, but made no attempt to turn away. Instead he began to stroke his cock slowly.

Rick worked his way down Alec's body until he reached his cock. He licked the underside of Alec's shaft a few times, and then turned into a sixty-nine position. They began to suck each other and Andy got harder and stroked faster. He was surprised that they stopped and didn't get themselves off. Minutes later he knew why. Alec took a tube of lube from the bedside table and generously greased Rick's ass and his own cock. Rick was on his back. He raised his legs and Alec placed his cock at the entry to Rick's love hole. He began to push in and he entered effortlessly. With Andy watching, Alec was so turned on, he came quickly and Rick was so hot, he did also. Rick's cum coated his stomach and Alec's cum was trying to seep out of Rick's ass.

Andy was shocked when his two hosts started to lick Rick's cum off his body and swallow it. Andy was so lost in lust; he had no idea what he was doing. He was standing over them desperately whacking off, trying to attain some relief. Alec saw him first. He pushed Andy's hand away and devoured Andy's cock in his mouth. When Rick was aware of what was going on, he got out of bed, and approached Andy from the rear. At first he thought he would fuck him, but he thought better of it and started to lick Andy's crack. Every time his mouth made a slight entry, Andy moaned and his whole body shivered. He came gushing stream after stream into Alec's mouth. Alec wasn't sure if he should, but he stood up and kissed Andy, passing Andy's cum into his own mouth. It came as a pleasant surprise that Andy kissed back, and swallowed what was offered him.

The three men lay down on the bed.

"That was awesome," Andy said. "I had no idea."

"You ain't seen nothin' yet," Alec said. After we recover somewhat, and maybe have a drink, Rick is going to fuck me. Keep your eyes open novice. You might learn a thing or two."

Andy reached out and fondled Alec first and then Rick. "I've never felt anyone's cock but my own before this," he said. "It feels so nice, so soft on the out side, and so hard on the inside. Thank you guys, thank you."

Rick reached for Andy's cock and it got instantly hard. "Would you like to try a little more gay sex?" Rick asked him.

"Absolutely," Andy answered. "At last, I'm not a virgin any more."

"Technically you are," Alec corrected him. "How would you like to be the lucky guy in the middle?"

Andy may have been a virgin, but he knew instantly what Alec meant.

"Take my virginity," Andy said. "Take all of it."

Tale Five: Under The Hollywood Stars

Andy had been staying with Rick and Alec for three weeks, and working at The Golden Cockerel as a bartender (one of his hidden talents) for almost the whole time. The three of them were enjoying an interesting and expanded sex life together. Often Marty and Tyler joined in on the festivities. The five young men were becoming fast friends. They were all sure that their special relationship would last a life time.

Then fate stepped in for Andy, in a good way. Early one evening, the bar was very slow. An exceptionally hot young Latino man came in, sat at the bar, ordered a gin and tonic, and said to Andy, "You are one hot guy. I sure would like to get into your pants."

Andy was flattered and answered, "I'm not nearly as hot as you are, buddy." Whenever Andy had a moment he would chat with the young man, whose name he learned was Carlos. He was still seated at the bar when Alec came in for his after gig drink.

"Hi Alec," Carlos said cheerily.

Alec didn't recognize the young man, and asked, "Do I know you?"

Carlos got hysterical with laughter and Alec could not figure out why. "I'm Miss Fantasy," Carlos said. "I guess you didn't recognize me."

"No way," Alec said incredulously. "I've never seen you out of drag. Why didn't you tell me how hot you were?"

"You never asked, gorgeous," came the reply. The three men chatted for awhile and Rick joined them after his shift. When Rick and Alec finished their free drinks, they left. Carlos stayed at the bar until Andy was finished at 2 AM, and then Andy went home with him. If ever there was a case of love at first sight, this was it. Two weeks later and three weeks before it was time to leave for Hollywood, Andy moved into Carlos's apartment.

Alec and Rick, Marty and Tyler and now Andy and Carlos bonded into a tight knit family unit, a real band of brothers. Since Rick and Carlos were to be American Idol widowers for the foreseeable future, they were glad they had each other.

All six of the brothers were at the airport to see Alec and Andy off to Hollywood. There was a lot of hugging and tears and well wishes. When they left the airport, Tyler and Marty returned to school and Rick and Carlos went to work. This was Miss Fantasy's night to entertain at The Golden Cockerel.

The big jet landed smoothly at LAX and Andy and Alec removed their carry on bags from the overhead. Neither had checked luggage. They took a cab to the hotel to which they were assigned. When they checked in they received an envelope informing them where to meet for dinner. They would be given further instructions at dinner. The weeding out procedure was to begin the following day. There were 140 contestants that would be weeded down to twelve for the live competition. Two contestants would be eliminated by public vote during the first two weeks of the competition. Those two weeks were critical because the contestants who made the top ten would tour the country after the competition and get paid for it. More importantly their talents would be exposed to the whole country.

At dinner that night, they were all instructed where to congregate for further auditioning. There was a huge auditorium in the hotel and they would be singing there with all the other contestants acting as a live audience. Andy and Alec immediately made a few friends at dinner. All of the girls and some of the men were attracted to their good looks. A handsome young man whispered in Alec's ear, "A few of us are going to a gay bar after dinner. If you are so inclined, please join us. Your room mate is welcome to come along, but my vibes are that he is straight."

Alec laughed. "His partner would be shocked to hear that."

The young man laughed, "I'm Matt," he said and stuck out his hand.

In all, seven of them went to the bar. They enjoyed one drink each and Alec said that he wanted to be well rested for the ordeal to come. He and Andy wanted to return to the hotel, which was walking distance from the bar. The others scoffed at them. It was obvious they didn't think they had a chance to make the cut, and they wanted to have as much fun in Hollywood as they could, before they were sent home.

"Are we the only ones taking this thing seriously?" Alec asked Andy, not expecting an answer.

There were two queen size beds in their hotel room. "What a waste," Andy said as he and Alec jumped naked into one of the beds. They assumed the position and played sensuously with each other's cocks. Finally they each engulfed the other and brought each other to glorious orgasms. They swallowed each other's cum and there was no waste. Afterwards they wrapped up in each other's arms and fell asleep. Their body time clocks were set for three hours later, and they were terribly overtired, so sleep came easily.

The next two weeks were grueling. Most of the time was spent just sitting in the audience and waiting. Alec and Andy made cut after cut, and found themselves in the top twenty-four. Only one day of competition remained until the top twelve were chosen. Alec had listened carefully to the judges' advice. They seemed unanimous in their opinion that his guitar playing was weak compared to his singing. They urged him to either drop the guitar or maybe just use it as an intro. Alec felt naked without his guitar, but he knew instinctively that he should take the judges' advice. Even if he didn't do as well without his instrument, maybe they would give him brownie points for listening to their advice. He decided that at this final audition, he would sing without his guitar. After all Andy was doing well enough without an instrument for a crutch.

The judges would often say to a contestant, "That was not a good song choice for you," and so now Alec was faced with a major decision. What should he sing? He tried hard to listen to his father's voice, and in a fleeting instant he heard, "Climb Every Mountain." He rejected it immediately. One of the judges was very disdainful of singers who sounded "Broadway." The judge felt that Broadway singers could not become super star artists. Alec thought that a Broadway song was not a wise choice.

Again he heard his father's voice, "Climb Every Mountain." He decided to go with it, and leave it to fate. At this final audition, he had a full orchestra at his disposal. He and the orchestra leader listened to several arrangements of the song, and Alec selected the one he liked the best. During rehearsals the two musicians made some changes to the arrangement, adding a crescendo here, and toning down another there.

Finally it was Alec's turn. He took center stage. One of the judges said, "I see you have no guitar today, Alec. Let's see what you can do without it. What are you going to sing for us today?"

"Climb Every Mountain," Alec said. The anti Broadway judge arched his eyebrows. The orchestra began to play a lush, string dominated introduction. When Alec began to sing, the judge's arched eyebrows became wide eyed wonder. One of the female judges began to cry. At the end, the remaining contestants, led by Andy, applauded wildly. They and the judges gave Alec a standing ovation.

That afternoon, the contestants were called into a private room one at a time to hear the judges render their final choices. Alec and Andy made the cut and were in the final twelve. They were given passage home, along with all the other winning and losing contestants. They had to promise not to reveal the results, because the whole selection process would not begin airing for another two months. If the results got out they would risk losing their standing, and would be replaced by a runner up.

On the trip home they wondered what they would tell their friends. They decided to tell them that they didn't make the cut, put up with their disappointment, and just go back to work. At the eleventh hour they would pack, say their goodbyes, and head back to Hollywood. That's just what they did. During the first few days they heard a lot of sympathetic mumblings from their friends and the bar patrons. They accepted these condolences graciously. Their partners felt that an abundance of sexual activity would ease the pain. Neither Alec nor Andy cared to disagree on that.

Alex and Andy both got through the first two cuts, which were decided by the viewers, and were in the top ten, assuring them a place on the tour. The night after the results, the other eight contestants went out on the town, but Andy and Alec decided to celebrate in their hotel room. They called their partners who were temporarily rooming together until Alec and Andy would come home. They then indulged in a night of wild, abandoned love making. Alec actually lost count of the number of times he entered Andy and spilled his juices deep inside Andy's ass. Andy chose to cum in Alec's mouth and to share his juices with Alec. He too came several times before they both collapsed in exhaustion.

The next few weeks were more hectic than before. In addition to rehearsing for the show the contestants would be making a weekly commercial together for one of the sponsors. It was incredible how hard they worked and how exhausted they were at the end of the day. Andy and Alec began to substitute sex for just falling asleep in each other's arms.

Before they knew what had hit them, Alec and Andy found themselves in the top five. Neither could believe that they were that good. Andy rationalized that all the young girls and probably gay men were voting for them because of their looks. They failed to give credit to their talents and their incredible charisma. After all they were both regional winners of local Fox TV affiliates.

They found themselves receiving requests from several agents to sign contracts with them to manage their careers. They were both promised record contracts and major gigs across the country. When they did go out on a rare evening, they were pursued by paparazzi, and had to run from them and screaming young women.

Finally, it had to happen. In the week before the grand finale, Andy was eliminated, leaving only Alec and a fantastic girl singer whose forte was rock. Alec was more of a balladeer. Do not cry for Andy. He was now a household name and a true American idol. He received several offers through his newly chosen agent (Alec's also) and after consultation with Carlos he agreed to go to New York to star in a revival of Oklahoma. Rehearsals were not scheduled to begin until after the tour so everything worked out perfectly. "It's my curly hair that did it," he announced. Carlos thought that he could advance his career in New York as well, and he was happy to make the move.

The top ten were all to appear on the final show and on the results show the following evening, so Andy stayed in LA. The night after he was eliminated, he and Alec were just getting ready for bed when there was a knock at the door. Alec quickly put on a pair of briefs and opened the door to find two smiling faces, Rick and Carlos.

"We're here for the finale," Rick announced. He started undressing rapidly as did Carlos. Andy and Alec were already naked. Each couple took a bed and made love far into the night. During the rest of the week they mixed it up a lot.

Rick and Carlos rarely left the hotel room. Andy left only for rehearsals. He was recognized wherever he went, and he didn't want the press to pick up even a hint of homosexual activity until after the last show. He feared that Alec's chances would be compromised if the public suspected that he was gay. Alec was so busy rehearsing and making the final commercial that he rarely saw his friends.

The finale consisted of each of the finalists singing a song of their choice, a duet together, selected by the judges, and a song written especially for the occasion. Alec dared not even hope, but the song each of them would sing was a ballad, and he thought that might give him an advantage over the rocker.

Between the guest artists, the top ten contestants and the two finalists, the two hour finale was a resounding success, one of the most entertaining two hours of television variety ever aired. The two finalists kept hugging each other. They were both winners. The "loser" would miss out on the cash award, but they were both already bombarded with recording and concert offers.

The only one who was neither excited nor happy was Rick. Alec's career was somewhere out there in the stratosphere. He knew that they would be immensely wealthy, but where did that leave him? He feared that Alec would move on without him, and he hadn't even finished high school. Well, neither had Alec, but no matter there. He vowed to finish high school and go on to college. He had always wanted to study law, and he swore that somehow he would realize his dreams. He was sure that Alec would help him.

He also knew that Alec would be on the road a great deal, and he wondered what that would do to their relationship. If he was in school, he would not be able to travel with Alec. Alec could sleep with groupies every night. Maybe Alec would get tired of him. Maybe Alec would think that he was boring.

Rick withdrew into himself and Alec was aware of it. After the finale, the top ten, the judges, the orchestra, and the guest artists had a huge back stage party. Carlos stayed away and Rick stayed with him. They had a quiet dinner together in the hotel. Carlos wanted to know what was bugging Rick. Rick was one to keep things bottled up and Carlos got very little out of him.

It was Alec who was able to put his finger on the problem. After the party, Andy joined Carlos in their hotel room, but Alec asked Rick to please join him for a night cap. Rick was not in the mood but he followed Alec down to the bar.

"Listen jerk," Alec said. "Get over your funk. I love you with all my heart and soul. You are never going to be out of my life. I know you are worried about me being constantly on the road, but that's bull shit. If you want me to promise fidelity, I will, but don't be stupid. We'll have long separations. I want you to be free to have sex with anyone, and I want the same privilege. You notice, I said, *have sex*. I didn't say *make love*. If you ever make love to someone else, I want to see you immediately, so we can discuss it. Do you understand what I am saying to you? You and I have mated forever. Don't ever doubt that for a second."

Rick nodded, and started to cry. "Alec," he said, "since you will be away so much, would it be OK with you if I went back to school? I want to study law?

"It's more than all right," Alec said. "I was going to suggest it. You were always the one with the brains. Your dad fucked you up. I want to make it right."

They finished their drinks and went upstairs. They were too tired for sex and fell fast asleep in each other's arms. Andy and Carlos were making non stop love in the other bed, and it didn't disturb them at all.

The one hour results show the next evening again featured the top ten finalists and guest artists. This time Carlos and Rick were in the audience. They both knew that success for Andy and Alec was assured. Of course, they wanted Alec to win, but they knew that some of the runner ups had eventually gained more success than the winners. They just relaxed and enjoyed the show. The hour dragged on interminably, but then the moment came. The huge audience became stony silent. The host took forever to open the envelope and then he hesitated for what seemed an eternity before he announced the winner.

"Alec Thomas."

Tale Six: Epilogue

Andy and Carlos went to New York. Andy became one of the brightest stars on Broadway. He starred in one musical comedy after another until finally he was lured back to Hollywood to star in a non singing romantic comedy. Carlos was never without a gig in New York, but like Rick, he went back to school, where he studied statistics. When he and Andy moved to California, he got a well paying job with a major insurance company. Andy was often tempted by handsome gay men in his industry, but his heart remained strongly with Carlos. Carlos gave up his drag career to be a full time statistician.

Marty and Tyler finished college and became CPA's. They started their own firm in Ft. Lauderdale, advertising heavily in the gay press. They never grew to be a large firm, but they were successful and lived a life free of financial stress in the city that they had grown to love.

Alec enjoyed a successful career in concerts and TV. His recordings often went platinum and he had more Grammies than he had room for on his shelves. He also won an Emmy for a TV variety special, and he actually did a cameo role in one of Andy's musical films. After that he appeared in a movie of his own, but it wasn't a comfortable venue for him, and he never made another film. Rick became a lawyer and was wooed by some of the best firms in the country. It was common knowledge that he was the partner of super star Alec Thomas, and these firms believed that his status would attract many clients. He chose a prestigious New York firm. He and Alec made New York their primary residence.

Once a year, come hell or high water, the six brothers took a week off and met at the Beverly Hills estate of Andy and Carlos. They spent the week naked around the pool. Carlos made sure that all the servants were young gay men. The brothers enjoyed sex amongst themselves all week, and often the young servant men joined in on the festivities.

One day, when Rick least expected it, he received a letter from his mother. He was shocked. It read:

Dear Richard.

I often see your picture in the paper with that handsome singer, Alec Thomas. My friends just adore him. I was able to trace you when I read that you now live in New York City. Your father forbids me to acknowledge that you exist. He remains ashamed of you.

I want you to know that I don't feel that way. I had to obey your father's wishes, but my heart is broken. I love you now as I loved you then.

I will be in the New York area without your father from Labor Day weekend until Sunday of the following weekend. My sister, your Aunt Clara, now lives in Cedarhurst on Long Island and I am spending the week with her.

I would so love to see you. Can you find it in your heart to forgive me and have dinner with me one evening? I'll be arriving Friday afternoon before Labor Day. Please call me on my cell phone Friday evening. The number is 207-555-3478. If I don't hear from you, I'll take it to mean you don't want to hear from me.

Your loving mother.

Rick cried for an hour and then called Alec, who was just finishing a gig in Atlantic City. Rick was crying so hard, Alec could barely understand him.

"I'll be home the entire holiday weekend," Alec said. We'll call her and meet them in the city on Saturday evening for dinner. You should see as much of her as you can during the following week while I'm away. This is wonderful news.

Rick, his mother, his aunt, and Alec met at one of New York's finest restaurants. The reunion was very tearful. Rick held his mother's hand all through dinner. He was busy working on a big case, but he agreed to go out to Cedarhurst for dinner at Clara's on Wednesday evening. The ladies were thrilled. Of course, Alec charmed both ladies. They were gushing all over the big star. Clara took pictures to show her friends whom she was certain would not believe this at all.

When they got ready to leave, Rick's mother kissed Alec. "Thank you for taking such good care of my son and for loving him," she said. Alec held her tight.

The ladies had come in to the city by railroad, but Alec arranged for a limousine to take them home. When they left the restaurant they were bombarded by flash bulbs. The paparazzi were out in force, but Rick tried to cover his mother's face lest his father ever see the pictures.

His mother pushed his hand away and defiantly said, as she looked directly into the cameras, "Let him see me, damn him."

That night as they prepared for bed, Alec took Rick in his arms. "We did good kid," he said.

"Yeah," Rick answered, "we did real good. We've come a long way from under that bridge."

THE TALES OF
THE COUNTRY CLUB

Tale One: Jamie Berman

BERMAN THE BARMAN

Jamie Berman was the bartender at The West Los Angeles Country Club. He was affectionately called "Berman the Barman," by the staff and members of the club. He was in his fifteenth year at the bar, and he worked every day except Monday. He took a two week vacation every year, and he had never missed a day for illness. He was at his station every day by 10:45AM and he opened the bar promptly at 11AM. Except for bathroom and dinner breaks, he was behind the bar until he closed it at 9:30PM. He served his last drink at 9:15PM. No matter how much a member begged for another, Jamie stuck to the rules (which he himself had established.) The club hired temps for special events, and for Jamie's vacation. The bar at the club was his own private kingdom, and everyone knew and accepted that fact.

Jamie was now thirty nine years old. His whole life was centered on the club. He knew every member, even those who did not drink. But more than that, he knew more about their personal lives than their spouses, their children, or their parents knew. He always said that he could write a book. Jamie was king of the gossips, or should I say queen? He was out and out gay, and never tried to hide it. He was a stereotype; flamboyant, a wild dresser, outrageous hair styles, embarrassing makeup, and more feminine than a Hollywood starlet. Both the ladies and the men loved to stop by the bar, have a drink and get treated to a little "dirt" about someone, straight from Jamie's lips. If he had some particularly juicy bit of gossip, it was all around the club in minutes and came right back to him in a whispered, "Did you hear…?"

At least two nights a week, when Jamie went to his car to drive home, there would be a male club member waiting for him to follow him home. Usually it would be a well married club member, who was stuck in the closet, and desperately needed the relief Jamie could give him. Do not believe for one moment that Jamie was a prostitute. He didn't expect payment for his sexual favors, but these people often left a "bonus" for him on his dresser.

And why not? Jamie was a handsome man, and once away from the club, he removed all his makeup, combed out his outrageously styled hair, put on a pair of shorts and a muscle shirt, and looked damn manly. He stood five feet, eleven lean hard inches. His hair was straight and black and hung down to his neck. His eyes were brown and when he looked at you, it was like Bambi pleading with you not to shoot his mother. His skin had an olive complexion. His body was hairless, because he shaved it entirely, including all his pubic hair. He kept his finger nails and his toe nails clean and well manicured.

The minute he got home every night, he showered and shaved. The perfume he wore all day disappeared to be replaced by the scent of manly cologne. Jamie stood in front of the mirror and admired himself. Not only did he apply the cologne to his fresh shaven face, but also to his body, paying particular attention to the area below his genitals. As he did, he watched in the mirror as his four inch, flaccid, cut cock began to sprout. As it approached its six and a half full inches, Jaime substituted the cologne for an unctuous body lotion. If he had company, he would then go into the bedroom fully aroused. If he was alone, he stroked himself with the body lotion until he shot forth in heavy gushing streams, coating a good part of the mirror.

FRANK AND PAUL

Recently Jamie had taken the virginity of three sixteen year olds who were sons of members. They were all good looking, but he was particularly hot for Daniel Sherwood, the son of Larry Sherwood, a long time member. But even more interesting, Daniel was the step son of Mark Cook, the club's gorgeous tennis pro. Jamie suspected that Mark was one of those closeted husbands. He had been trying to get Mark into bed for years without success, so when Daniel showed an interest, he was right there. Maybe he could get the stepfather through his stepson.

Daniel was already taller than Jamie was, and his big cut cock was also bigger. Daniel was almost fully grown and quite mature for his age. By pre-arrangement, Daniel cut school one Monday and drove to Jamie's apartment for some fun and games. Daniel suspected that he might be gay, but when Jamie took his virginity that day, all his doubts were removed. He knew from that day forth that he was a committed homosexual. The two men indulged in oral and anal sex for hours. Jamie made sure that Daniel's first experience would never be forgotten. Poor Daniel could barely walk to his car later that afternoon.

Jamie was also fucking two other boys and none of the three knew about the other. First there was Frank Carillo, who was about five feet, five inches, pleasingly plump, with a three inch uncut cock, that barely made it to four inches hard. He would grow some more, but he was maturing at a slower rate than Daniel. Then there was Paul Lassiter. At five feet, eight inches tall, he was somewhere between

Daniel and Frank. His cut cock was huge, the biggest of the three, easily ten inches erect. Jamie let Paul fuck him and he bled for two days, but he was getting used to it, and now he couldn't get enough.

None of the boys knew about the others and they swore Jamie to secrecy because none of their parents knew, and they were very closeted in school. Jamie wasn't about to break his youthful golden eggs, and he kept his mouth shut. His gossipy nature hungered to spread the word around the club that these three boys were gay, but he controlled himself. Instead he decided to be a matchmaker and fix the boys up together. He couldn't care less if two of them hooked up, or all three. If that suited them it would be all right with him. Jamie's life was skewed enough. He never judged others.

The boys usually came over on different Mondays, and Jamie's adult tricks usually followed him home from work at night. When he began to fixate on matching up the boys, his mind began to churn about fixing up some of his adult friends also. They were mostly all married and in the closet. He reasoned that they might welcome meeting other men with whom they could play. It would certainly give him a break. Poor Jamie was approaching his fortieth birthday and his body was telling him to slow down.

He started with the boys. He invited all three over on the same Monday morning. Each boy was thrilled that he wouldn't have to wait the usual three or four weeks to fuck Jamie or get fucked by him. Jamie always used oral sex for foreplay, and the boys loved everything he had to offer them. He drove them so wild with his well experienced tongue that they usually begged to be fucked afterwards. He always kept them in suspense by insisting that they fuck him first. They were young and easily erected again after Jamie's blow job. By the time he got around to fucking them, they were begging for it.

On the Sunday before the meeting, Daniel approached Jamie at the bar, and told him that he was seriously seeing someone, and he wouldn't make their rendez-vous the next day. Jamie was surprised, but happy for Daniel. He tried to find out who the lucky fellow was, but Daniel was mum. Anyway, Jamie felt that Paul and Frank would be a good match, and it would be easier without a third teen ager present. He told Paul to arrive at 9AM and he told Frank to arrive at

9:15. He didn't want them to run into each other until they came face to face in his apartment. The boys went to the same high school and played tennis together at the club, but neither was aware of the other's attraction to men.

By the time Frank arrived, Jamie and Paul were playing a hot game of sixty-nine in bed. Frank was on the verge of cumming for the first time that morning. He was moaning so loud that Jamie didn't have the heart to stop, but when the doorbell rang, he stopped sucking Paul, who then groaned in agony. Jamie pretended to be annoyed. "Shit, who the hell can that be?" he asked the thin air. He got up, threw on a robe, and went to the front door, leaving Paul with a severe case of blue balls. He pulled Frank inside and locked the door again. Then loud enough for Paul to hear he said, "For Christ sake, Frank, you weren't supposed to be here this week. One of us screwed up, but as long as you are here, you might as well join us. Come into the bedroom."

Frank looked surprised but he followed Jamie into the bedroom. When he saw Paul and Paul saw Frank, both jaws dropped. Frank spoke first. "Paul Lassiter," he said, "you are such a jock. I can't believe it."

Paul recovered quickly. "Frank, you little butter ball, get your ass in bed with us so I can grab those luscious looking love handles." Frank undressed quickly, jumped into bed, and lunged at Paul's cock. He had never seen a cock that big and he immediately hungered for it. The boys got so wrapped up in doing each other that they never noticed Jamie slip out of bed and get dressed. He went into the living room leaving the two boys alone.

Frank practiced everything Jamie had taught him on Paul. He sucked Paul's cock like a seasoned homosexual. Paul's blue balls were a thing of the past in no time. Then Frank fucked Paul. Paul had to really tighten up his ass muscles on Frank's immature cock, but he did a great job and he gave Frank the ultimate pleasure. The two boys were so thrilled at having discovered each other, and to have a convenient fuck buddy, that afterwards they kissed and fondled each other, trying to show the other how happy and content they now were.

They no longer had to wait for every three or four Mondays to have sex with another human being.

When Jamie stopped hearing noises of love making, he peeked into the bedroom. The two boys were basking in the after glow. They had wrapped their arms around each other and they were tongue kissing all over the place. He heard Paul whisper to Frank, "I wish I had known sooner. We've wasted too much time." They resumed kissing and fondling each other. At some point they finally realized that Jamie wasn't in bed with them. They called for him and he went into the bedroom.

"What's up with you, Barman?" Paul asked.

"Nothing, I just wanted you two to get together. Honest, you don't need me anymore. Now play with each other as much as you want, and I'll bet you'll meet others at school. If I learn about anyone else at the club, I'll certainly let you know." He thought of telling them about Daniel Sherwood, but Daniel was *involved*, so he said nothing.

The boys were somewhat disappointed, but they both knew that this day was inevitable. Frank thanked Jamie for fixing him up with one of the handsomest jocks in school, and Paul thanked him for fixing him up with the cuddliest teddy bear in the senior class.

The hardest thing for Frank and Paul after that was finding the time and the place to get together. Both parents spent a good part of the day at the club on Sundays. They played golf and then showered and dressed and had dinner at the club, but usually not together. The boys usually spent the day with them. They would have a tennis lesson, play tennis and then spend a good part of the day at the pool. What excuse could they use for staying home on Sundays?

They each told their parents that they were inundated with senior school projects and needed some quiet time at home, but both agreed to join their folks for dinner at the end of the day. As soon as their folks left, one of them drove over to the other where they practiced on each other, and became accomplished gay lovers. After awhile, Frank could take Paul's humongous cock without any pain at all. In time, the two boys actually fell in love and started making plans to go to the same college. Many of their classmates were planning on

going to Berkeley and that's where they both applied to attend. They
were accepted and arranged to room together. Soon they could make
sneaking around a thing of the past.

Berkeley had a large population of gay students, and Frank
and Paul came out to their classmates, if not their parents. They
joined a straight/gay alliance and that's where they ran into Daniel
Sherwood, their former high school classmate. They soon learned
that Daniel was sleeping with several members of the alliance. They
hadn't cared for him in high school and they didn't socialize with him
at Berkeley either.

Belatedly, Frank began to grow by leaps and bounds during
their freshman year, and he soon surpassed Paul in height by a half
inch. His cock grew a couple of inches, but it never achieved the
length and girth of his lover. It didn't matter to either one of them.
As a result of his growth spurt, Frank lost his excess fat, and he and
Paul made a handsome couple indeed. They made love often, but
each acted as a monitor for the other, making sure that each kept up
with his studies. They grew deeper in love each day, and it was not
uncommon to hear one of them whisper into the wind, from time to
time, "Thanks Jamie, for introducing us."

When Paul's humongous tool was inside of Frank, he was
particularly grateful to Jamie.

TOM AND PHIL

When the boys all left at once to go up to Berkeley, Jamie was at a loss to find any other teen agers to take their place. There was one other boy who Jamie was sure was gay, but at eleven he was way too young. Jamie would bide his time until the boy started to give him hints. In the meantime, Mondays became his day of rest once again.

You would think that there wouldn't be more than one or two closeted married men, who had sought to bed down with Jamie, but in truth there were five. Balancing his schedule became a delicate matter with Jamie. He had to maintain a regular appointment book. Three of the men could not get away regularly, and they only visited him sporadically, but Tom Harris came over every Tuesday evening. He told his wife that it was his poker night. She never asked where the game was, and she was grateful that he never asked her to allow him to host the game in her house.

Phil Carriere was a dedicated visitor on Sunday evenings. He travelled all week on business, so he told his wife he had to leave Sunday night in order to make early Monday morning meetings. In truth, he spent Sunday night with Jamie, and he left Los Angeles early Monday morning. He never scheduled a meeting until after lunch on Monday, giving himself enough time to get from the airport to his business appointments.

Jamie noted that both men played golf on Saturday, and that sometimes they were matched in a foursome together. On Sundays, they played tennis with their wives and were sometimes matched against each other. Jamie would chuckle to himself and wonder what each would think if they knew that he was fucking both of them, and they were both fucking him. It struck him even funnier, when after a mutual golf game, they would both come into the bar for a drink, and he would serve them with his usual friendly face, but without any hint as to their intimacy.

It further struck him as downright hilarious, when they came into the bar with their wives after having played tennis together. He would serve all four, and openly flirt with the ladies. The wives were flattered even though they knew that Jamie was harmless. He would look at them and wonder what they would think if they knew that their husbands were fucking him and he was fucking them.

On school holidays, when Frank and Paul came home, they would let him know how happy he had made them. On their last visit, they even told him that they were getting ready to come out to their folks, because they couldn't bear to be apart when they were home from school. It got Jamie to thinking. He wondered if Tom and Phil would be as happy, if he got them together, and they didn't have to depend on him so much. He began to plot how to do the deed. It was not possible to schedule them on the same night as he had done with the boys. He racked his brain, dreaming up the most intricate scenarios, none of which seemed feasible.

In the end, he came up with a simple solution. Without mentioning names, he would tell each one that there was another club member in a similar situation to his. He would reveal that he was screwing both of them. He would then indicate how compatible he thought they would be together, and he would ask if they would like to meet the other. The plan was almost too simple. Before acting on it, he spent many more hours looking for any loop holes in his planning that could possibly hang him and his two fuck buddies. He couldn't find any, and it seemed the only way to go.

He saw Phil first on Sunday night. He allowed Phil to be particular passive that night and he did all the work. He brought Phil to orgasm with his tongue and his lips, and Phil reported one of the most intense orgasms he had ever had. It encouraged him to beg Jamie to fuck him. Jamie had no objection to that. Afterward,

Phil was happy and exhausted. Seeing how mellow Phil was, Jamie broached the subject.

"Look Phil," he said. "You shouldn't always count on me for relief."

"I don't," Phil answered.

Jamie was shocked. "What do you mean?" he asked.

"I make out on the road sometimes."

"You devil," Jamie laughed. "How would you like to have a steady fuck buddy at home? Someone you can socialize with and not raise any eyebrows?"

"You know somebody for me?" Phil was more than curious.

"Let's just say that there are other men at the club who have the same hunger and the same needs that you do. In fact I am seeing several of them, and there is one guy in particular that I think you should meet and get better acquainted with." Jamie winked at Phil and Phil knew exactly what Jamie meant by "get better acquainted."

"Are you interested?" Jamie asked. "If you are, I can arrange it."

"Hell yeah, I'm interested," Phil exclaimed. "Who is he? Do I know him?"

"I told you. He's a member of the club and you know him, but I won't tell you his name unless he agrees to meet you also. I'll be seeing him Tuesday night."

"You've really got me excited," Phil said. "I'll be in Phoenix on Wednesday. I'll call you from there. Now let's get some sleep, I've got an early flight tomorrow."

That Tuesday night, Jamie gave Tom the same loving treatment he had given Phil, and when Tom was coming down from a very intense orgasm, Jamie presented him with the same proposal. Tom agreed immediately and pressed Jamie for his potential lover's name, but Jamie said that nothing would be revealed until they met. Jamie pointed out to Tom that the hardest thing would be to find a mutual time when they could both get away from their wives.

"Do you want to meet here or in a hotel?" Jamie asked in all sincerity.

"I don't know about Mr. X," Tom replied, "but I think here would be the best place. You better have some stiff drinks available. I'm suddenly very nervous about this meeting."

Phil called early the next morning before Jamie left for work. Jamie explained that the other guy could only come over on a Tuesday evening and it was Phil who came up with a solution. "I'll take two days off, and book only Wednesday to Friday. I'll tell my wife that I am flying out Tuesday night instead of Sunday night."

"That sounds like a plan that will work," Jamie commented.

Phil had already booked the next two weeks, including his flight tickets, so Jamie arranged the meeting for three Tuesdays hence. Again he told them to arrive fifteen minutes apart, but this time, he did not have sex with Tom who arrived first. Instead they waited expectantly for Phil. When he came in the two men did a double take. At first they giggled awkwardly, but then Tom stood up and embraced Phil. The two men looked in each other's eyes for a long time. Finally Phil said, "I've always had the hots for you." The two men burst out laughing and then they kissed each other very passionately.

Jamie said, "I'll leave you two alone. You know where my bedroom is."

When they were alone, Tom said to Phil. "It's hard being married and knowing that you are living a lie. I ache every day."

"Tell me about it," Tom commented back. "There are many nights I cry myself to sleep."

"Me too," Phil said. He took Tom's hand and led him to the bedroom. Jamie prepared to camp out on the living room sofa that night. He was smug in the knowledge that he had made another match.

In the bedroom, the two men undressed each other slowly and methodically, until at last they stood facing each other naked. They loved what they saw. They were both in their early forties, and their bodies were toned and their skin was tight. Neither was too muscular, but they were both lean and attractive. Tom was six feet, two inches tall. He had dark brown eyes, medium brown hair and a light smattering of hair all over his body. His pubic hair was bushy and plentiful, and Phil decided to ask him to trim it somewhat. His cock was simply beautiful. It was about five inches flaccid and rather thick. He was uncut, but he did not have excess foreskin. The tip of his sheathe barely covered his head. Phil could not contain himself. He reached out and took Tom's cock in his hand. It immediately erected to about seven inches.

Phil was exactly six feet tall. Unlike Tom he was quite hairy. His legs and back were furrier than most men. Fortunately Tom liked hairy men. The thick hair on Phil's chest especially excited him. Phil's hair was black and his eyes were blue. His skin was very pale and it made his blue eyes appear almost luminous. Some people would say that he had bedroom eyes, whatever that means. His cock was about the same size and girth as Tom's, but he was cut. As soon as Tom's cock erected in his hand, Phil's cock did also. Tom grabbed for it.

The two men fondled each other for awhile, and then fell into bed. They twisted into a sixty nine position and went to work. There is nobody hungrier than a man who is in the closet and living a lie, and then at last he is doing what nature intended him to do. Phil and Tom ravished each other. They came, panting heavily, into each other's mouths. They both swallowed all they could and then kissed passionately; blending what seed each had left. They hugged, fondled and kissed, crying and laughing alternately. Finally Tom realized that he needed to get on home. He envied Phil, who could sleep over until it was time to go to the airport in the morning.

When he was dressed, Tom gave Phil his business card. "Please call me at my office from the road. We have so much to talk about," he said. The two men embraced and Jamie literally had to pull them apart so that Tom could leave.

Phil and Jamie slept in the same bed that night, but didn't have sex. Jamie lay still beside Phil basking in the knowledge that he had made yet two more men very happy. His mind was already trying to figure out who else he could hook up. He suddenly concluded that it was his calling to be a matchmaker. It never occurred to him to think about himself. After all, he was no spring chicken.

JAMIE AND DANIEL

When the three teen agers, who Jamie was having sex with, went off to college, Jamie found himself missing Daniel, but not Paul and Frank. He would dream about the boy, and yearn for him. But now Paul and Frank were a couple and Daniel had told him that he was "involved," so he put all three of them out of his mind and concentrated on his adult "friends" at the country club. Jamie's work schedule did not allow him much of a social life and he depended on these guys for his needs as much as they depended on him. His efforts were commendable, but as much as he enjoyed match making, he was diminishing his pool of fuck buddies.

Then something unexpected happened. When Daniel's freshman year ended, he showed up at the bar one afternoon and ordered a gin and tonic. He was more than legal now and Jamie happily filled his order. There were a few other club members at the bar, but they soon left. When they were alone, Daniel told Jamie that he had been miserable and home sick at Berkeley. He told Jamie that he was transferring to UCLA for next semester.

"I wanted to live with my dad and Mark," Daniel said, "but for personal reasons we all agreed that it wouldn't be too wise a move, so I am living with my mom and her new boy friend. Confidentially, I think he'll be out of the picture soon."

"What about the guy you were involved with?" Jamie asked. "Can't you live with him?"

"Oh," Daniel lamented, "That relationship has been over since I graduated high school."

Daniel lowered his voice and leaned into Jamie. "I'd really like to see you again and soon," he whispered.

Jamie smiled. "You know when I get off work, and you know where I live. If you come over tonight, I'll be waiting."

Daniel gave Jamie a smile and a thumb's up. "I'll see you later," he said, and he left. Jamie could barely perform his duties the rest of the day. He was happy to stay behind the bar because it helped hide the constant erection he got whenever he thought about Daniel's impending visit.

That night, they made love like they never had before. They warmed each other up by sucking each other's cocks in a hot game of sixty-nine, but they managed to avoid cumming. Then they alternated fucking each other. It was a record breaking, marathon night. Jamie came twice, and Daniel exploded inside Jamie three times. They shared the knowledge with each other that neither could remember having more intense orgasms.

That summer, Daniel stayed over at Jamie's apartment almost every night. It was an unlikely liaison, and as much as both men tried to stop what was happening, they were falling deeply in love.

"I'm twenty-one years older than you," Jamie kept protesting.

"I don't fucking care," Daniel protested in return. "I never related well to people my own age. That's why I was so unhappy at Berkeley. All I could think about were you and M..." He stopped himself short.

"You were about to reveal the name of the guy you were involved with," Jamie said.

Daniel nodded and said, "My lips are forever sealed."

Jamie's gossipy nature and his overwhelming curiosity took over his reason. "If you really love me enough to share your life with me," he challenged Daniel, "you'll tell me who it is, and you'll trust me to keep your secret. If you don't, I won't believe you love me, or trust me, as much as you claim."

Jamie was right of course. If you love someone enough there should be no secrets between the parties, and they should trust each other to keep those secrets from others.

"I promise you, if you ever tell a living soul, I think I'll be mad enough to murder you. You absolutely must keep my secret to prove your love for me, and my trust in you, and in our relationship," Daniel said.

"I swear," Jamie almost screamed. "Tell me before I die."

"I was making it with Mark Cook while he was still married to my mother."

Jamie's jaw dropped open and for a change he was at a loss for words, but not for long. "Son of a gun," he murmured. His lips were barely parted as he spoke. "I tried every trick in the book to get him into my bed. Even though he was married, I just knew he was gay." Jamie looked at Daniel. "Well I landed a bigger prize, and a much better one. I got his step son."

"Imagine how I felt," Daniel said. "He dumped me for my father. If that wasn't bad enough, I thought my father was totally straight, but the night I came out to him, he told me that he was bisexual. Obviously, he's all gay now."

Jamie started to laugh. "What's so funny?" Daniel wanted to know.

"I swear nobody will ever know. I thought that keeping the identity of my club member tricks was hard for me to do, but this will be even harder. I love you and I'll do it for you, but what I am laughing at is an image I just had of running into your two dads at some gay bar, or even double dating with them. Can you imagine going out to dinner with them?"

"Actually I can," Daniel said, "but let's not be premature. I think our relationship will take some getting used to on their part. Let's be patient and not push it."

Before the semester began, Daniel moved in with Jamie. When his tricks from the club learned that he was in a monogamous relationship, they were more than frustrated, but they were happy for him.

Daniel's mother was not happy at all. She had sent her latest lover away, her daughter had just left for an out of town university, and now she was alone for the first time since she had married Daniel's father, Larry. There was little she could say to keep Daniel in her home since he was of legal age, and Larry was paying the college tuition for both their children.

Larry and Mark were a little upset at first about the age difference between Daniel and Jamie, but when they saw how happy the two men were, they relented and approved. In fact, they took the happy couple out to dinner to celebrate. Jamie never believed that it could happen, but who better could understand their love than another gay couple.

As for the members of the West Los Angeles Country Club, they lost their most colorful employee, not literally, but symbolically. Jamie gave up his flamboyant demeanor. He no longer wore makeup to work. He combed his hair fashionably but conservatively, and he wore appropriate attire for anyone tending bar. In order not to be tempted to blurt out his remaining secrets, he stopped gossiping altogether. In time, there were no juicy stories making the rounds at the club, and it appeared that all the members were squeaky clean.

Paul and Frank, Phil and Tom came around regularly to report on their status. Both couples seemed to be getting closer to each other all the time. It didn't even disturb Jamie that Phil and Tom were talking about divorcing their wives and moving in together. He felt it was the proper and honest thing for them to do, so why should he be upset in any way.

Paul and Frank came out to their parents. They all suspected anyway, and it wasn't as bad an experience as the boys thought it would be.

Every day, Jamie said to himself, "All's right with the world. I am with a wonderful person whom I love dearly." He would then say a small and silent prayer thanking God for his good fortune, and by the way, for the gift of love he had been able to give to others.

Tale Two: The Tennis Pro

It was mid morning on a beautiful Sunday in Los Angeles, and I was still sound asleep. I don't remember what I was dreaming, but I do remember being rudely awakened by the shrill ringing of my bedside phone. I reached for it groggily, and tried to read the caller ID. While I was engaged in trying to focus my sleepy eyes on the phone, I heard a grunt. Lying beside me, on top of the bedcovers, was a gorgeous young man. He didn't look to be of legal age, and I groaned. My teen aged son looked older than he did. He was in his birthday suit, and he had a humongous cut cock. He was practically hairless. I could hear him breathing, but I had no idea who he was. Worse, I had no recollection of having had sex with him the previous night, if indeed we had engaged in sex at all.

It struck me that lately I had awakened too often to find a nameless body sleeping beside me. Ever since I divorced my wife, or more accurately, she divorced me, my life has been a series of drunken one night stands with both men and women. I am an equal opportunity fucker, sometimes the fuckee.

My eyes finally focused in on the caller ID screen, and I was surprised to see the name, M Cook. Mark was the tennis pro at my country club, but more importantly, he was the guy my wife married after she dumped me. I was glad to be free of Karen when she left me, but I did not have high hopes for her second marriage. Karen is a stunner, and she looks much younger than her thirty-nine years, but still, Mark is ten years her junior.

"Hello," I mumbled. I waited expectantly. I was more than intrigued by his call.

"Hey Larry," I heard. "It's Mark Cook."

"Yes?" I asked with a question mark in my voice.

"I'm Sorry to bother you," he said. "I'm at the club. I was wondering if you could come by for lunch. It's on me." I said nothing and there was silence. Finally he added. "I really need to talk to you."

I grew concerned. "There's nothing wrong with my kids?" I asked in alarm. My son Daniel is nearing seventeen and my daughter Jordana is about to have her sixteenth birthday. Both my kids live with their mother and Mark.

"No, no, nothing like that. I just need to speak to you. I can't talk about it on the phone. I'd really appreciate if you would have lunch with me today."

I grumbled my acceptance and hung up the phone. I needed to pee badly and relieve my morning wood. I tried to get out of bed without disturbing sleeping beauty. I crept to the bathroom and locked the door behind me. I examined myself in the mirror, and was not pleased to see what I saw.

I had a two day growth of beard, and black circles under my eyes. I looked a real mess, but the rest of the image pleased me. I stood five feet eleven, and possessed a lean hard body. My blue eyes were still blue, but a bit red at the moment. My hair was straight and dark blond. I remember when I had platinum blond kiddy hair. My chin was square and strong. My cock was cut and hung below my balls. It was probably five inches flaccid and seven inches hard. I never measured. I smiled in the mirror as I thought to myself that I didn't look more than a few years older than my son. He was a clone of me except he was two inches taller. He got his height from Karen's father. He had a slight scar on his left cheek from where the doctor turned him in Karen's womb when he was born. Actually it made him look manlier than I did. I still had a very boyish appearance. I knew he was cut like me, but I couldn't help wondering how big his cock had grown. I hadn't seen him naked since the last time I took him in the shower with me, just before his fifth birthday.

I shit, showered, brushed my teeth, and shaved. I was probably in the bathroom for about a half hour. When I returned to the bedroom, my bed mate was gone. I looked around quickly, and could not discern that anything had been taken. I would never know who he was, but at least I knew that I had good taste.

I was partly wrong. I found a note on the dresser. It read:

Dear Mr. Sherwood: Thanks for a wonderful evening. You are a great lover. Jake. Well, I now knew that I had indeed had sex with the boy, but I still didn't know who he was. I groaned when I read *Mr. Sherwood.* Jake must have viewed me as an old man.

I proceeded to dress for my luncheon date with Mark. Even though I had brushed my teeth, my mouth still tasted like morning after shit, so as soon as I dressed and straightened out my bed, I went into the kitchen and poured myself a tall glass of orange juice. It would have to do me until I could sit down with Mark for a meal. Hoping to cure my hangover, I vowed to have a scotch, straight up, as soon as I got to the club. I locked up the house and drove my car out of the garage.

Traffic on the freeway was very heavy, and I figured it would be an hour or more before I could get to my destination. I didn't have Mark's number, but I called the reception desk at the country club and left a message for him that I was running late. Stuck in the impossible Los Angeles traffic for long stretches at a time, I had plenty of time to reflect on the events leading up to what might be an interesting meeting with Mark Cook.

I had always been a jock in high school. I was tall, blond, handsome, and a two letter man. I was besieged with young women (girls really) who wanted to lose their virginity with me. I had no trouble obliging them. When most of my friends were still using their fists for sex, I was already a seasoned veteran. I continued my successful run with the women in college.

Early in my freshman year, my room mate came out to me. I was surprised to learn that he was gay, but I was big about it and very liberal, and I let him know that it made no difference to me or to our friendship. Jared was handsome and athletic, and did not fit any of the gay stereotypes. He often walked naked around our dorm room, so I knew that his flaccid uncut cock was at least an inch bigger than mine. I wondered how big it was when he got hard.

We got drunk together one night and when we got back to our room, we both stripped completely. I lay down on my bed and Jared pretended to pass out right on top of me. I don't know if he knew what he was doing, or if he did it in a drunken state, but he began to seduce me. His hands were all over my most private parts. I was more than curious, and he was arousing me, so I allowed myself to taste the forbidden fruit. I figured it was a one time shot and I wanted to experience it all, so I gave Jared as good as I got from him, both anally and orally. I discovered that he was thicker and longer than me when he was hard. That man's dick was a beauty. Afterwards, lying in his arms as he slept, I realized that it didn't take a genius to tell me that the man to man sex I had just experienced satisfied my needs far more than any sex I had ever had with a woman. I continued to have sex with Jared and with many women (no other men) until graduation. I knew that as much as Jared satisfied me, I wasn't going to complicate my life by living it as a gay man.

Lucky for me, I met Karen at my first job. I landed a great position with an electrical engineering firm, and Karen was my boss's secretary. She was a real beauty. She had long brown hair, hazel eyes and a figure that wouldn't quit. Her tits were firm and neither too large nor too small. I adored her upturned nose and the few freckles along the bridge. She slept with me on our very first date, and to my delight she liked to do things I had only done with Jared, and which no other women wanted to do with me. Yes, some of them enjoyed sucking my cock, but none to date liked anal sex and certainly wouldn't permit me to do it to them. Karen, on the other hand, practically begged me for it. On her part, she was pleased that I didn't balk at anal sex, or get turned off by it. I can't honestly say that I loved Karen, but I knew I would never find a better sex partner among the ranks of the female of the species. We got married when I was twenty-four and she was twenty-two.

When my son Daniel was on his way, Karen resigned her position and became a full time mother and homemaker. Daniel was born two weeks shy of our first anniversary when I was a young twenty-five year old yuppie.

My firm grew by leaps and bounds, and in a few short years I made partner. As my income grew, we bought a new home (a very large one) and once we settled in our up scale neighborhood, we joined the country club most of our neighbors belonged to. We were living the American dream. I really don't believe that we appreciated our good fortune. We just thought it was our due.

When Mark came to work at West Los Angeles Country Club, Daniel was just eleven years old. The first time Karen saw the tennis pro, her heart skipped a beat. He was a six foot tall handsome athlete. His wavy black hair was almost ebony, and it accentuated his pale skin and sky blue eyes. His chin was strong and his body was hard. His short, short tennis shorts left little to the imagination concerning his package. Karen had always been a great tennis player, but she immediately enrolled Daniel in a beginner's class just so that she could get to know Mark better. She made up her mind to seduce him.

At the time she met Mark, she had been cheating on Larry for three years. When they had been married for nine years, she decided that she was bored, and needed a variety of men, with their different sizes and techniques, to satisfy her. Larry had many opportunities to cheat, but he stayed true to his wedding vows. One of his coworkers was gay and out, and Carl often joked with him about how much he wanted to go to bed with him. Larry was tempted, but he remained loyal to Karen. Even so, he remained good friends with Carl, and often had lunch with him.

When Mark first laid eyes on the young eleven year old Daniel Sherwood, he had trouble controlling his rising cock. The boy was almost as tall as he was, mature for his age, and exceptionally handsome. He knew that the boy was way out of bounds, and he started to teach him with decorum and restraint. When it would even have been obvious to the village idiot that Karen was coming on to him, Mark encouraged her advances. He saw it as an opportunity to be close to Daniel. He made it his mission one day to have sex with Daniel.

So it wasn't very hard for Karen to bed Mark, and they began to have sex regularly. Unfortunately the only time he saw Daniel was at tennis lessons, and those times were sporadic at best. Mark used every trick in his book to keep Karen satisfied and wanting more. He was very successful, and one day, nearly a year after they started to have sex, Karen announced that she was leaving Larry and wanted to marry Mark. Mark was shocked. He certainly didn't want to marry Karen, but he knew that marriage would mean that he would be living in the same house as Daniel. He gave in to Karen's pleading, and did as she wanted. He was actually giving in to his desire for Daniel.

Five years of marriage went by quickly. Daniel was now nearly seventeen years old and Mark's lascivious desires were becoming an obsession with him. There were many times when the two men were alone in the house together, and Mark would talk to Daniel about sex, and would ask him about his love life, which was almost non existent. Daniel often neglected to lock the bathroom door when he was in there, and Mark would "accidently" walk in on him. Daniel would object strongly and Mark would leave. He tried to arrange a fishing trip just for him and Daniel, but Daniel nixed it, stating how much he hated fishing. Mark was getting desperate.

His obsession had a ripple effect. He was paying less and less attention to his spousal bedroom duties, and Karen's eyes were wandering again. She had gone back to work as a secretary, and she started to have an affair with a co-worker. Mark sensed what was going on, and fearing that he would lose Daniel, he began to pay more attention to Karen. It was too late. She was too smitten with her co-worker.

Mark knew that Larry had been through the same experience and he decided to call him and seek his advice.

———————

The traffic began to move slowly and I snapped out of my reveries. I wondered what Mark could possibly want to talk to me about. As long as it didn't concern my children, I wasn't too worried. I wondered if he, or maybe Karen, was sick. I couldn't care less if it was so. I would be glad to offer my kids a home even if it would impede my sex life. Traffic halted again, and I began to think back to my life since Karen left me.

———————

Larry didn't have sex for nearly two months after Karen and he split up. One day he let Carl talk him into having dinner with him that night. Larry was honest enough with himself to fear what might happen. He remembered the wonderful sex he and Jared had enjoyed in college. He was afraid that he would finally give in to Carl and go to bed with him. Well that would be fun, he concluded, and he wondered what he was so fearful of.

Carl wasn't the beauty that Jared had been. He was maybe five feet seven, and a wee bit plump. Larry also knew from sightings in the men's room that Carl's cut dick was no more than three inches flaccid. Still he might be a grower and not a shower. None of that mattered. Larry really liked Carl. He was a kind and gentle man, cute and cuddly as well.

Sure enough, he and Carl had sex that very night and many times after that. Carl pushed for a commitment, but Larry wasn't interested. Instead he hopped from one sex partner to another. He was oblivious to which sex he slept with. He just wanted to have fun.

In the meantime, Mark's obsession to have sex with Daniel was becoming morbid. He was losing all reason. He and Karen were planning a big party for Jordana's sixteenth birthday. Jordana was a very popular kid and the guest list was overwhelming. Fortunately everything was being catered in the back yard, so there was plenty of room. About an hour before the party, Daniel went upstairs to shower and get dressed.

Mark followed him, and when Daniel went into the bathroom, he waited until he heard the water running in the shower. He slipped into the bathroom and locked the door. He removed all his clothes and entered the shower. Daniel had not heard or seen Mark because of the cascading water. To say he was shocked would be putting it mildly. Before he could question or object, Mark took Daniel's cock in his hand and started to stroke it. The feel of the cut seven inch beauty aroused Mark to his limit of hardness.

How difficult is it to seduce a seventeen year old boy? Daniel's cock grew harder and extremely luscious in Mark's hand. Daniel began to moan and Mark took it as a good sign. He fell to his knees and took Daniel's cock into his mouth. His tongue ran up and down the underside of Daniel's dick, and his lips pulsated sensually on the base. It didn't take Daniel long to cum convulsively in Mark's mouth.

Mark grew frightened because of what he had done, but he needn't have. Daniel raised him up and began to kiss him. At the same time, Daniel fondled Mark. Daniel was amazed at how thick and long Mark's hard cock was. Now it was Daniel who fell to his knees and went down on Mark. Before Mark could cum, Daniel stood up and turned his ass to Mark. "Fuck me," he demanded, and Mark soaped his cock really good and entered Daniel easily. Mark suspected that Daniel might not be a virgin. Several short jabs later, Mark unloaded up Daniel's ass. Afterwards the two kissed passionately and Daniel whispered in Mark's ear, "What took you so long to seduce me? I was getting ready to turn the tables on you." They laughed, cleaned each other up, and got dressed for the party. After that they had sex often, but when Mark realized that he was losing Karen, he feared he would lose Daniel as well. He decided to call Larry for advice. He didn't want to make the same mistakes Larry had. He wanted to keep Karen, or rather, Daniel.

I entered the bar at the country club and immediately ordered a scotch and soda. After the first sip, I asked the bartender, Jamie, to please have Mark paged, and let him know that I was at the bar waiting for him. Jamie was openly gay. I didn't like how he smiled and winked at me when I asked him to page Mark. Did he know something I didn't know? He paged Mark, and five minutes later, Mark came into the bar with his hand extended. We shook hands and stared at each other. I rarely interacted with Mark, and I had forgotten how handsome he was. We were both speechless and I could see that Mark was looking at me strangely.

Mark was awed at the strong resemblance my son had to me. I didn't know it at the time, but he immediately hungered for me as he had hungered for Daniel. Fortunately, my sex life was private, and he had no reason to believe I was anything but straight. He was wondering if he could seduce me, and it left him speechless.

Finally we both found our tongues. "I've reserved a quiet table in the far corner of the dining room," he said. "We'll be able to chat privately."

"OK," I mumbled and followed him to the dining room. The maitre d' seated us in a far corner, and I could see that we did indeed have our privacy. The table was a small table for two. Instead of sitting opposite me, Mark moved his chair around to sit at right angles to me.

I guess one of my eyebrows raised up, because that prompted him to say, "I want to speak to you confidentially. If I whisper, you'll be able to hear me better." All I could do was nod and grunt.

He said nothing to me until after we placed our orders, then he leaned into me. When he did that our knees touched, but neither of us moved away. "I'm losing Karen," he said. "I'm pretty sure she's having an affair with some guy in her office. I know this will sound crazy to you, but you've been through the same thing. I don't want to lose her, and I thought you could offer me some advice from your own experience, which might help me."

I was stunned, but when it all sank in, I started to laugh. "Forgive me for laughing," I giggled, "but I'm the wrong one to ask for help. I had no problem giving Karen up. I don't think I ever really loved her. It was all about the sex." I paused and I could see the disappointment on Mark's face, so I leaned right into him. Our knees were now grinding harder together. I whispered in his ear, "You fuck her in the ass, don't you? It's her favorite thing."

"That's not the problem," he whispered back. "I ass fuck her more than the other way."

"Well, she needs a lot of sex," I suggested. "Sometimes she would bug me for it two or three times a day. Luckily I was young, like you are now, or I couldn't have kept up."

The look on Mark's face was unmistakable. It was a look of pure guilt. "I've got something on the side," he whispered in my ear, "and I may have neglected her a little."

I was shocked, but I put on my wise face, and said, "There you go. I am able to help you after all. Give up your side activities and concentrate on your wife." Mark looked pained.

"I wish I could," he said, "but I can't. I need them both." I could tell that he wanted to tell me something more, something even more confidential, but I could also tell that he wasn't going to reveal any more to me. I thought that he might do so at a later time, but not now. What more could I say?

"If you want to hold on to Karen, I guess you will have to have enough stamina for both women," I mumbled. His mouth opened up, and for a brief moment I thought he would reveal more to me, but he clamped shut his lips.

After lunch we shook hands and parted. As I left him I said, "I'm really sorry I wasn't much help to you. All I can do is wish you good luck."

"I hope we can see each other again soon. I'd like for us to be friends," Mark said, looking sheepish.

"Yes," I answered. "That would be nice. I'd like that too."

******

About a week later, I got a call from Daniel just as I was leaving my office. He didn't ask, he begged me to have dinner with him that evening. He said that he had an important matter to discuss with me. I had plans for dinner and sex with Carl that evening, but I cancelled, much to Carl's chagrin.

Daniel met me an hour later at his favorite barbequed chicken and rib joint. As soon as we were settled at our table, I asked him what was so important. He looked uncomfortable and said, "Dad, I really don't want to discuss it here. After dinner could we go to your place and talk in private?" Now I was really intrigued. Neither of us lingered long over dinner.

When we arrived home, Daniel settled into my big lounge chair and I made myself a scotch and soda. I offered him a coke which he turned down. I sat down on my sofa facing him. "OK," I said. "Shoot!"

Daniel sat upright on the lounge. "Dad," he declared, "I'm gay."

Daniel was a jock like me, and frankly I was shocked. I still did not identify myself as gay or bi sexual. I considered my dalliances with men to be pure fun and games. I guess he left me speechless which prompted him to say, "You hate me, don't you?"

It was as if a knife went through my heart. I jumped up and went over to him. He stood up and I embraced him. He started to weep and he put his arms around me. "Dumb ass," I said. "I could never hate you. I would love you no matter what. Do you think I give a fuck who you sleep with?" Lightening struck and I added, "Have you had a gay experience yet?"

"Yes Dad. In fact that's why I told you. I'm in love with an older man. We have sex often, but he's married, and I don't know what to do."

"How much older?" I asked for no particular reason.

"About twelve years."

"I've already told you that I can accept that you are gay. What do you want me to say about your older lover, who is married to boot? I certainly don't approve. You should be looking for someone your own age, and available."

"I know that, Dad," "but I love him. I want to be with him all the time, but because of circumstances that's not possible. And for the past week, I have hardly seen him. He seems to be avoiding me."

"Chances are that he'll never leave his wife for you or any other guy. You have to give him up son," I said. I tried hard to keep calm. Then I went out on a limb. "Listen to me," I said. "Since your mother and I split, I have been having nothing but recreational sex. I rarely see anyone twice, and I am just as apt to wake up with a strange woman in my bed with me as a strange man. I swing both ways. I have fun, and the last thing in the world I want is a goddamn relationship. Who needs it? I have sex several times a week, and don't ever suffer the pangs of love." As I said those words, I thought of Mark Cook. I felt a stirring in my groin, and I was shocked at the thought.

Daniel was staring at me. "You have sex with men?" he asked. Had I really admitted it to him?

I nodded and asked him if he had ever had sex with a girl. He shook his head. "I like both sexes," I repeated. Daniel didn't know what to say so he just hugged me.

"I'm glad you confided in me, son. Does your mother know?" I asked. Daniel shook his head. "When you are ready to tell her, let me know. I can be there with you if you like?"

"Gee Dad that would be great." He hugged me tighter.

"Another thing, young man," I said sternly. "You're jail bait. I could talk to this cheating SOB and scare the shit out of him."

"Oh, please don't," Daniel pleaded. "I know he could go to jail for having sex with me, but that would hurt his wife, and I don't want that on my conscience."

"Then promise me that you'll stop seeing him."

"I'll try."

In the days that followed I could not lose the picture of my own son having sex with an older man. The other guy remained faceless to me, but I grew more and more curious as the days flew by. Often in the throes of passion, that image would come to me.

On the following Sunday, I invited Carl to golf with me at the club. We were in the bar after the round, and just as we clinked our glasses containing our first drinks, Mark walked in. He spotted us and he came right over. We shook hands and I introduced him to Carl. I could see the look of lust in Carl's eyes. He asked Mark to join us. I wasn't happy about it, but I couldn't say anything.

Carl only had the one drink, and then said that he had to leave. His folks had invited him to dinner that evening and he had accepted. He left me alone with Mark. As soon as Carl was out of the bar, Mark said to me, "Daniel told me he came out to you, and you were very supportive. That left me in no position to be otherwise. How do you really feel about it?"

"It's none of my business who Daniel sleeps with. I just don't want to see him hurt. Did he tell you about his older, married lover?"

"Yes," Mark nodded. "I told him what you told him."

"And what was that?" I asked.

"Give him up. Look for someone your own age. Don't get serious. Have sex for fun. Try it with a girl. All that stuff. But he told me that neither he nor his lover wanted to give each other up."

"That's lousy," I said.

"He also told me that you have sex with men as well as women," Mark said in a conspiratorial tone of voice.

"Damn that kid," I pretended to be angry. "I told him that in strict confidence."

We were still seated at the bar, but Mark put his hand on my knee. It was rather very much in the open, but I didn't stop him. "Don't sweat it man," he whispered. "I do it too. I think most men try it one time or another. I find it very, very satisfying."

I was springing a boner. I have already told you how attracted I was to Mark. I don't know where I got the courage from, but I asked him, "Would you like to go to my place if you are free."

He smiled, "I'm very free. Karen won't be home tonight. I think she is seeing her lover. Let's get out of here. I'll follow you in my car." As we left, I could swear that I saw Jamie, the bartender, smirking at us.

When I got to my house I pulled my car into the garage, and Mark parked in my driveway. He got out of his car and followed me into the garage. I closed the overhead door and before we could even enter into the house we were all over each other, kissing and trying to undue our belts.

"Please," I said, "let's go inside." Once we were in the house we calmed down a little. I led Mark to my bedroom where we stripped and dragged each other into my bed. It turned out that Mark was much more aggressive than I ever was. He threw himself on top of me and started kissing me passionately while fondling my balls. Damn!! It felt good. He was rough. Not so rough as to hurt me, but rough enough to get my juices going. I kissed him back hard, and then I surrendered completely to him. I sensed that was what he wanted of me.

He kissed his way down my body as I lay back, very passive. His kisses were accompanied with little nips at my skin. I shivered with delight as he went lower and lower. He reached my balls and managed to get both of them in his mouth at once. He suckled for a long while and I thought I was cumming. He sensed it also. He withdrew and slathered his tongue up and down my crack, and when my moaning grew too loud, he transferred his tongue to my cock, and nibbled on it. It was a while before he started to stroke it with his tongue. Then something happened to me that had never happened before.

I felt my orgasm building, but it wasn't in my crotch. It seemed to be welling up in my toes and then in my fingertips. It travelled slowly through my body and finally reached my cock. Not only was my cock spasming, but my whole body was. I felt my orgasm in every cell of my body. The orgasm took forever to climax, and then it did not seem to cease. Long after I had stopped ejaculating, I continued to orgasm throughout my whole body. Thankfully it just went on and on.

I tried to warn Mark when I was cumming, but I couldn't breathe and I came gushing down his throat. He swallowed it all. He kept my cock in his mouth until it was mush. Then he retrieved his pants and removed a lubricated condom. He put it on and stood between my legs. I just smiled at him and wrapped my legs around his waist. Positioning his cockhead at my manhole, he pushed in slowly. He penetrated so slowly that I hardly felt when he went past my sphincter. I didn't realize that he was all the way in until I felt his pubic hair against my ass cheeks.

"Fuck me," I tried to yell, but I was shocked at how weak my voice sounded. "Fuck me," I said again, accepting the child like sound of my voice. He fucked me hard, and came too quickly for my taste. I so wanted more of him. Well, he was young. Maybe he could fuck me again after some rest.

He collapsed on top of me and we hugged and kissed for what seemed forever. I was surprised. Usually after sex, if I was sober, I was anxious to clean up and either leave my trick or have him/her leave me. Then again nobody had ever affected me the way Mark just did. I found myself content to lie in his arms and snuggle with him. I wanted to stay this way all night. I could only wonder if this could be love when Mark whispered in my ear, "Dammit, Larry Sherwood, I think I love you. I don't want to go home. I want to stay here all night with you, no matter what the consequences."

All I could do was utter in a guttural voice, "Stay, Mark. I really want you to stay. I think I love you too. This is a fine mess we have gotten into."

"It's worse than you know," Mark said.

"What do you mean?" I asked. Mark got off of me and sat up in bed. He took my hand and held it.

"First, let me tell you that I'd be happy to spend the rest of my life with you," he said. "I fell in love with you that day I asked you to have lunch with me. Please believe that. Like you, I never really loved Karen. I married her for the sex, but not her sex. I wanted to be close to Daniel."

I pulled my hand away from him. "Are you.... are you the older married man my son is sleeping with?" I tried to put a lot of spite in my voice, but I couldn't. It just came out as an ordinary question. Mark just nodded and started to weep.

"I never touched him until a few weeks ago," he said, "when he had just turned seventeen. He went out of his way to be naked in my presence, and he never locked the bathroom door. He tempted me beyond my endurance. We both wanted it. I swear."

I suddenly grabbed Mark and embraced him to reassure him that I still loved him and wanted him. "Well, that puts Karen on the back burner as a problem for us," I said, "but what the hell are we going to do about Daniel?"

"Nothing," Mark said. "I'll just tell him that I'm too old for him and break it off. Karen and I will be splitting soon, so that will make it easier for both of us."

"That's all well and good," I commented, "but what happens when he finds out that we are a couple? I don't know if I can share him with you."

"You won't have to. He's going up to Berkley in a couple of months. He just might meet someone there. Let's not do anything to rock the boat until he leaves."

"That sounds good, but you'll have to fuck Karen and Daniel during that time. Where does that leave me?"

"I told you," Mark answered, "I'll break it off with Daniel and avoid sleeping with him. Karen has a lover and she'll probably kick me out any time now. I just don't think we have a problem. I guess that means that I should probably go home now and ride it out."

"I think so too," I said.

"When will I see you again?" Mark asked.

"Whenever you can. I'm all yours," I answered him.

———————

Daniel graduated from high school three weeks later. He had been solemn and morose ever since he came out to me. I got him alone after the ceremony and asked point blank what the matter was. "My lover won't see me anymore," he said. "He broke it off because of our age difference. I know that's nonsense. It must be something else."

"You'll be fine," I said. "Your mother left me, and I'm doing great. When you go off to college in a few weeks, I just know you'll meet lots of great guys." I told him about me and Jared, but I don't think he looked any more relieved than he had before my little speech.

That night Karen made a graduation party for Daniel. She introduced me to a good looking man from work. I could tell that he was a few years younger than she, and I was certain that he was her new heart throb. That night, after the party, she asked Mark to leave. He packed a couple of suitcases and she said she would send the rest of his stuff to him when he got settled.

First he knocked on Jordana's door to say goodbye. She couldn't care less that he was leaving. Jordana was still sulking over my departure. Then he went into Daniel's room without knocking. He assured Daniel that he would stay in touch with him. "You can always reach me through the club," he told my son. That having been said, he drove straight to my house.

Thank God the next day was a Saturday. Mark and I had made love all night, and I couldn't get out of bed. Poor Mark had several lessons to give that morning and he dragged his ass out of bed and to the club. He came home after his last lesson and went right to bed. While he was napping, I decided to surprise him with a homemade dinner. I was puttering in the kitchen, when there was a knock at my back door. Daniel was standing there looking ghastly.

"What's wrong?" I asked him.

"Mom kicked Mark out."

"I know," I told him.

"No, you don't know," he protested. "Mark is... was my lover."

"I know," I repeated myself.

"You know? How?"

"He told me."

"And you didn't kill him?" Daniel asked incredulously.

I laughed. "No," I said. "You see Mark and I love each other and we are going to live together." Daniel started to say something, but I held up my hand to stop him. "We both love you very much. Never doubt that, but what you have with Mark is an infatuation and what he had with you was an obsession. What he has with me is love. I'll make you a deal," I said. "If I give you one last night with Mark, will you promise me that you will give us your blessings and try to find happiness with someone your own age."

"You would do that for us?" he asked.

"Yes, I think I can talk Mark into it."

"Talk me into what?" a voice behind us asked. Mark had come into the kitchen totally naked. When he saw Daniel he tried to cover himself, but he realized the absurdity of the situation, and Daniel and I broke out laughing.

"I promised Daniel one final night with you in return for his blessings," I answered Mark's question.

Mark looked at Daniel. "You know that I would do anything for you, *son,* but your father is asking me to do something very pleasurable in order to receive your blessings, so there's no problem." Then he looked at me. "I don't suppose you would care to join us?" he asked.

"Yuck," I said. "No that would be way too weird."

"Yes," Daniel agreed, "too weird."

Mark ran upstairs to put on clothes. It turned out to be a pair of boxers. The three of us busied ourselves making dinner. I called Karen and told her that Daniel was sleeping over. After dinner, we cleaned up. We embraced in a three way hug, and Mark and Daniel went upstairs to the master bedroom to say their farewells. I opted that night for the guest room.

I tried not to listen, but I could hear their love making all night. I was tempted to join them after all, but I resisted.

After that night I never slept with anyone else but Mark. Carl was devastated, but I told him it was time for him to settle down and find someone for himself. As for Mark, he had plenty of temptations at the club, but he came home to me every night, and he always assured me that I was the only one he wanted or needed.

Tale Three: Strange Bedfellows

They met in what was a pure act of fate.

The massive airliner lost a motor (the reason was investigated but never resolved.) The plane kept losing altitude as it approached the Rocky Mountains. The passengers could not have suffered, nor could they have known what hit them when the airliner smashed into the mountain and blew up in a massive ball of fire. Most of the victims were burned to a crisp and were never identified. A memorial service was held for the 225 victims in a small town close to the crash site.

James McIntyre, widower of one of the victims, sat in the third row. His two sons Thomas, 10, and James, Jr. (Jimmy), 6, sat to his left. Kate Fallon, widow of another victim, sat to the right of James. Her sons Ryan, 10, and Sean, 6, sat on her right.

Before the service began, the grieving adults introduced themselves, and offered condolences. They both lived in Los Angeles and both their spouses were returning home from business trips. They had each driven to the memorial with their two sons, and both families were staying at the same hotel, hoping to start for home early the following morning. James, in pure sympathy, asked Kate if she and her two sons would like to join his family for dinner that evening. She hesitated for a moment and then accepted. She felt that the company of someone who shared her grief would be much better than the company of someone offering condolences, but who could not possibly understand what she was going through.

The two families were shy with each other at first, but the boys started to talk about school and what they were doing and the atmosphere warmed up quickly. Kate and James became comfortable with each other also, but not until dessert. Ryan told a joke that was making the rounds of fifth graders in his school, and everyone actually managed to laugh. Tom said that the same joke was making the rounds in his fifth grade class also, and James remembered that this particular joke was popular when he was a fifth grader. They all laughed at that as well.

"Nothing unimportant changes," he observed, "but the important things in life are as inconstant as the moon." He quoted Shakespeare. Everyone nodded in agreement.

Both families returned to Los Angeles without having exchanged telephone numbers. Two weeks later, the baseball season was due to begin and James decided to take his two boys to Dodger stadium for the first home game of the year. He hoped it would help get them out of the depression they were in since losing their mother. On a lark, he looked up Kate Fallon in the phone book (of course she was still listed under Timothy Fallon) and he asked her if he could take her two boys to an upcoming Dodger game. She accepted at once.

When James came to her door on a Saturday morning two weeks later, Kate was dressed to the nines. James gasped. He hadn't realized how beautiful she was. The last time he saw her she wore no makeup, and her eyes were red and swollen. He couldn't help himself. "Wow," he uttered.

"Hi there," Kate greeted him. She saw his surprise and offered an explanation. "I've got myself a part time job at Nordstrom's. I'll be working from noon to six today. Do you think you could keep the boys until then? I usually get a sitter, but since you were taking them to the ball game today, I didn't bother."

Still stunned, James said, "Only if I can take you all out to dinner tonight."

Kate smiled graciously and said, "That would be really nice, Mr. McIntyre."

"James," he corrected her.

After that day, James became a surrogate father to the Fallon boys. He enjoyed that role and really wanted to do it, but at least on a subconscious level, he did it so that he could see Kate. He took the Fallons wherever he took his own boys, sporting events mostly, theme parks, museums etc. The boys all became close friends and they started having sleepovers at each other's houses. Both houses had a guest room, and whichever two boys were the guests slept there.

About eight months after the fatal plane crash, James took a quick shot of scotch and asked Kate out on a date. She accepted immediately. The McIntyre boys slept over at the Fallon's that night so that they only had to hire one baby sitter. After bringing Kate home, James went back to his house and he slept alone in the empty house.

Two years after the mutual deaths of their spouses, Kate and James were married in a simple civil ceremony. Their parents and their sons were the only guests. When they asked the boys where they would like to go for the wedding dinner, they all voted for Burger King, but the grandparents prevailed and arrangements were made at Wolfgang Puck's. The next day, Kate's mother came to stay with the four boys, and Kate and James went to Hawaii for a week's honeymoon.

One year after the wedding, James legally adopted Ryan and Sean, and their names were changed to McIntyre. There was never a hint that the boys were STEP brothers. They were true brothers. They fought like siblings do, but they loved each other dearly. The older boys, of course, considered the younger boys to be a complete nuisance and tortured them unmercifully. Notwithstanding that, all of them would sacrifice anything for each other.

Shortly before the wedding Kate and James sold their houses, and bought a large four bedroom home with an oversized den and a large maid's room off the kitchen, which they turned into a computer room. There were actually six computer stations in the cramped room, one for each member of the family. Every bedroom in the house had its own bathroom. There was also a downstairs bathroom next to the maid's room and a powder room off the main hallway entrance. Tom and Ryan, now twelve, shared a large bedroom with twin beds, and Sean and Jimmy, now eight, shared an equally large bedroom. The master bedroom belonged to the parents, and the fourth bedroom served as a guest room, mostly for visits from James' and Kate's parents.

For fifteen years the family lived inconspicuously on a quiet, tree lined street. The older boys were now twenty-seven and the younger boys were twenty-three. When Jimmy and Sean graduated from college, got jobs, and an apartment of their own, Kate and James were empty nesters. They sold the house and bought a more practical condominium.

By now Ryan was living in New York with his bride. He worked for a large commercial real estate management company. Tom was living in San Francisco. He was still single, and was chief accountant for a large retail clothing chain, which served both sexes. After graduation Sean and Jimmy got jobs locally and decided to share an apartment until such time as their status would change. Jimmy was seriously dating a young lady who was a senior at UCLA. Sean wasn't seeing anyone in particular. They took a modest one bedroom apartment that each of them could afford on his own should one of them get married and leave. The four brothers stayed in close contact with each other. They called each other often and texted and E Mailed each other whenever they could.

For all eyes to see, the McIntyres were an ideal American family, except that Sean had a secret. He felt that it was a secret he could never reveal. It became a great burden to him and a terrible cross to bear. At first, he didn't know what to make of it, but by the time he was twelve, he realized that he was gay. He successfully squelched his true nature, even from Jimmy with whom he shared his home and his life, at least for the moment.

During his growing up years, every time he saw Jimmy naked (which was often), he grew a boner. He had to hide it, and he would often run into the bathroom and whack off so that his libido could subside somewhat. He and Jimmy would often talk about sex as growing boys do, and when the time came they admitted to each other that they both whacked off, but they never did it together, and never saw the other do it. However they did participate in circle jerks with their friends outside the family. They were never in the same event.

When Jimmy asked Sean to share an apartment temporarily, Sean was really hesitant. It took all his will power not to tell Jimmy how he felt about him. In the end, he gave in. Somewhere buried deep in his subconscious was the hope that maybe something might happen between them. On a rational level, he knew that could never be.

Jimmy and his girlfriend decided to get married shortly after her graduation. The reception was held at the West Los Angeles Country Club where the McIntyres and the bride's family had been members for many years. It was a huge affair, and the whole family was together again. Ryan came from New York with his pregnant wife, and Tom came from San Francisco. Sean was Jimmy's best man. Sometime during the dinner, between the courses, the toasts and the speeches, Sean wandered over to the open bar. Tom was there also, and to tell the truth, both men were five sheets to the wind. When Tom had arrived at the airport he took a cab directly to the church. His suitcase was actually stashed behind the very bar the two brothers were standing at.

Jamie Berman, the club's chief bartender, seldom worked private parties, but he knew the McIntyre boys and the bride and her sister for most of their lives. He insisted on being in charge for Jimmy's wedding, and both families felt in good hands with Jamie behind the bar. His first order of duty was to refuse to serve Sean and Tom any more booze. He felt that they had enough. Jamie was the mother hen of the country club.

The two brothers hadn't actually had a chance to greet each other properly until now. They embraced and when Sean was ready to let go, he was surprised that Tom continued to hold him tightly. "I really miss you guys so much," Tom sobbed, and continued to squeeze Sean tighter.

"Ryan and Courtney are staying with Mom and Dad so do you think I can shack up with you tonight?" Tom asked.

"Absolutely, I'd love to have the company," Sean answered. "It'll be lonely tonight without Jimmy," he added.

The immediate family was the last to leave. Jimmy, and his new bride Jeannie, were staying in a hotel that night and then flying out the next day for London and Paris. They would be away for two weeks.

Kate and James made Sean and Tom promise to come over to their place the next day for lunch and to spend the afternoon with them and their brother and his wife. Tom's plane was to leave the next evening and James said that he would drive him to the airport. They promised to come to their parents the next day, and then took a cab to Sean's apartment.

Sean showed Tom to the bedroom and indicated which twin bed was his for the night. Tom stowed his suitcase and announced that he wasn't the least bit tired and asked Sean if he could have a beer. Sean retrieved two bottles of beer from the fridge and they went into the living room.   Sean sat on the sofa. He expected Tom to sit on the easy chair, but he was surprised when Tom sat down right next to him.

Tom's shoulder was pushing into Sean's, but they drank their beers in silence. After several minutes Tom rested his head on Sean's shoulder. Without thinking about what he was doing, Sean put an arm around his brother and held him tight. Tom nestled further into his younger brother and laid his arm high up Sean's thigh. Sean became very aroused, but made no attempt to hide his burgeoning cock. Instead, he whispered into Tom's ear, "You know, don't you."

"I don't know anything," Tom answered. "I'm only guessing. "Do you know how much I wanted you when we were living in the same house? I used to whack off constantly dreaming we were going at it."

Sean held Tom tighter, but he began to laugh. "Please don't laugh," Tom said. "I'm in agony."

"I'm not laughing at you," Sean assured him. "It's just so funny. I felt the same way about Jimmy, and it was worse. We shared a room and then an apartment and I had to suppress how I felt about him."

"Do you think that you could ever feel that way about me?" Tom asked in a whisper.

"I love you as a brother, but I don't know if I could make love to you. I'm not sure I could have done it with Jimmy either. It's just too weird."

"We are brothers emotionally," Tom said, "but technically, we aren't blood. When you love someone as much as I love you, why can't it be expressed physically also?" Tom asked.

"Tom," Sean said, "I'm almost twenty-four and I have never slept with anyone, male or female. I think I'm scared, but I wouldn't be scared with you."

Tom leaned over and began to kiss Sean. His hand travelled further up Sean's thigh until it rested on his crotch and caressed the hard cock he felt. They were both fully dressed. At the same moment they both put their drinks down on the coffee table.

"Let's try and see where it goes," Tom suggested. They stood up and undressed, dropping all their clothes on the living room floor. They had seen each other naked as boys many times, but never with hardons and never as young men. Their eyes soaked each other up.

Tom was six feet even. He was hard and muscular from long workouts in the gym. His hair was sandy blond. He had green eyes, and a pug nose. He was saved from looking too boyish by a square chin with a slight cleft. His body was almost hairless, as was Sean's. His uncut cock was almost seven inches hard, and currently it was dripping pre cum on the carpet. Sean was about an inch taller, but he wasn't as solid. Sean was a runner. He jogged many miles a week. He had brown hair, brown eyes and a straight nose. His chin was manly but rounder than his brother's. He was cut and about the same size in length and girth as Tom's. Tom and Jimmy were uncut, and Sean and Ryan were circumcised. As children this was always a big joke between the four of them. This joke was shared with nobody else.

"Have you done this before?" Sean asked.

"Many times," Tom answered. "I made most of my contacts at the gym. They were almost all one night stands. It was hard for me to get involved with anyone because you were always on my mind. I'm pushing thirty and I have never found true love because of how I feel about you."

Those words went straight to Sean's heart. He wrapped his arms around Tom and placed his lips on Tom's. He made no attempt to part Tom's lips, but Tom was not so shy. Before he knew what happened, Sean's tongue was dueling with Tom's and their hard cocks were pounding together.

"Let's shower," Tom suggested. I stink from booze and I don't feel clean." Moments later they were standing under running warm water.

"God, this feels good," Tom said. He was soaping himself, but suddenly he reached out and enveloped Sean's cock with a soapy hand. He started stroking Sean gently and Sean began to purr like a kitten.

"This is the first time anybody has touched me there besides myself," Sean uttered above the noisy cascading water.

"I am so happy to be the first," Tom said. At that moment he fell to his knees. He took Sean's anxious cock in his hand and allowed the running water to wash away the soap. Then he ran his tongue up and down the underside of Sean's pulsating penis. His saliva and Sean's precum merged into an ointment of honey tasting fluid, and Tom took Sean into him. Sean did not wish to cum so quickly, but he couldn't stop himself. After just a few short strokes, he gushed into Tom's waiting and expectant throat. Tom milked out every last drop until Sean begged him to stop. Sean was panting for breath and Tom stood up to support him and keep him from falling.

"You swallowed it," Sean said in amazement. "What does it taste like?"

"Your jism tastes like the nectar of the gods, but not everyone tastes the same."

"I want to taste yours. I need to taste yours," Sean said.

"No," Tom said, totally surprising Sean. "We are both a little drunk. I want you aware and in total control when we do more. I want you to be sure that this is what you want. Let's go to sleep and see how you feel in the morning."

"I won't feel differently," Sean said.

"Nevertheless!!" Tom reiterated.

They slept together in Sean's bed. Their naked bodies were wrapped so tight that they hardly took up more room than a single person would have. At about 4 AM Sean got out of bed to pee. As he stood at the toilet bowl, Tom came up behind him and wrapped his arms around Sean's torso.

"I need to pee also," he whispered in Sean's ear. Sean smiled and stepped a little to the side so that he and Tom could pee together. Sean finished first and brushed his teeth while Tom eliminated a lot of last night's booze. When Sean was done, he handed the toothbrush to Tom.

"I didn't expect company," he said. "I don't have a spare toothbrush."

After he brushed his teeth, Tom returned to bed. Sean was waiting for him and they began to kiss passionately. Sean began to work his way down Tom's body. He wanted all of his brother's body. He kissed his ears, his neck, his nipples, his innie, and reached Tom's pubic hair. He ran his hands through Tom's thick bush. Then very tentatively his tongue found a drip of Tom's precum. He was overwhelmed by the musky smell of Tom's pubic area and the sweet taste of his juice. He could bear it no longer and he took Tom into him. He sucked wildly yet gently and Tom began to squirm.

"I'm cumming," the elder sibling announced, and Sean took him deeper into his mouth if that was possible. When Tom let forth his first gush with a muffled cry, Sean withdrew a bit so that he could taste his brother's offering. He swallowed it all and only released Tom's cock when he felt it softening. He slithered up and positioned himself beside Tom.

They lay together silently for a little while and then Sean said, "That was beyond my wildest dreams, but I want to try the other stuff."

"What other stuff?" Tom asked as if he didn't know.

"Fucking," Sean stated in a matter of fact way. "I assume you've done it before and you can instruct me."

"Instructing you will be my pleasure," Tom laughed.

As much as they would have liked to have languished in bed all day making love, they got up, showered and dressed, and spent the day with their parents, Ryan and his wife.

Sean wouldn't let his father take the three visitors to the airport. He insisted on doing the honors. He dropped Ryan and Courtney off first. Then he parked the car, intending to wait with Tom until it was time for boarding. They sat in the car for awhile before going into the terminal. Sean was near tears. Tom was containing himself and he was squeezing Sean's hand so tight, Sean wanted to scream, but he didn't want Tom to stop.

"Now that we've found each other," Sean cried, "I can't let you go. What can we do? I want to be together with you."

"How tied are you to your job?" Tom asked.

"Not very," Sean replied. "I've been at entry level since I got the job. It took several months after graduation to land the position and so I've only been at it about four months."

"If I found something for you in San Francisco would you be willing to move?"

"In a heart beat," Sean said enthusiastically. "What did you have in mind?"

"My company runs an executive training program once a year. From that program they hire buyers, department managers and so on. Is that something you'd be interested in?"

"God yes," Sean answered. "You know that I'm a people person."

"The training starts next month. I know I can get you into it. I'll let you know for sure as soon as I know. In the meantime feel free to drive up or fly up any time."

Sean started to cry again and Tom reached over the console to kiss him.

"Life is so strange," Sean said. "I wanted Jimmy so badly and instead I fell in love with his big brother. Our big brother," he corrected himself.

"I love you too," Tom said. "Soon we'll be together forever."

Four weeks later, Sean drove a small U Haul trailer up to San Francisco. He had been on a month to month lease. He paid the landlord what was necessary to vacate the apartment, donated most of the furniture to charity, and headed north with no ties behind him except his parents, Jim and Jeannie. But they belonged to Tom also, and neither one of them was giving up any family ties.

Tom helped Sean unload the trailer and return it to a U Haul franchise. Tom had a one bedroom apartment also, but his bed was king sized. As soon as all of Sean's belongings were stowed, Tom ordered him to strip and get into the oversized bed. It was late Friday afternoon and Sean was not beginning his executive training until Monday morning.

"We aren't getting out of bed until we have to get up on Monday morning," Tom announced, "not even to eat."

"Yes," Sean agreed. "Let's spend the weekend fucking and sucking. Let's make up for lost time."

"Don't be so anxious," Tom said. "There's no urgency. This, dear brother, is the first day of the rest of our lives." With that having been said, he leaned over Sean and took Sean's cock into his mouth. Thus began a love making marathon that lasted forty-eight hours. Not once in all that time did either brother say, "I love you." They didn't have to. They had loved each other since they were little boys, and loving each other was simply implicit. No words were necessary between them.

A Boner Book

Tale Four: Summer Romances

PART ONE

School let out on June 15th and would not reopen again until the Monday after Labor Day. This summer was shaping up to be the best summer the Smiths had ever had together as a family. John and Jane had been married for fifteen years, and they were both thirty seven years old. They married on the weekend they graduated from college. They had two children Brett, 14, and Tiffany, 12. The family occupied a large five bedroom home, on a huge wooded lot, in an upscale neighborhood, on the south shore of Long Island, NY. They had only just been transferred from Los Angeles, less than a year earlier.

John was a big pooh bah in Bowers and Franklin, a Manhattan based investment company located in the financial district. The firm had branch offices in Los Angeles, Toronto, London, Paris, and one soon to open in Stockholm. A year ago John had been promoted to a vice president position. Along with that honor, came a big raise and a move from his home town of Los Angeles to managing the main office in New York.

John was sitting at his desk on a day late in April, trying to placate an unhappy client, when his secretary slipped him a note that Mr. Bowers wanted to see him. John told the client that it was difficult to review and advise her on her portfolio over the phone, so he set up a meeting with her two days hence, and went right over to Bowers' office.

He knocked on Bowers' door and heard the boss yell, "Enter." Bowers was on the phone, but he motioned John to be seated. John could see that his boss was having difficulty ending his conversation, but finally it was over. He buzzed his secretary and said, "No calls, please, until John and I are finished talking." Then he turned to John.

"I'll be brief," he said curtly. "The Stockholm office is opening sometime during the third week of June. I have every confidence in the Swedish crew we have hired, but I want you to go out there for the summer, and make sure they do things the Bowers and Franklin way. After all, it's a branch office, not a separate enterprise, and I want unanimity. As soon as school ends, I'm sending you out there with your whole family for the summer. I figure that your guidance should be over, and you can be in position to leave for home by the time school starts up again. At worst, you'll have to stay a week or two after your family goes home."

"Wow," was all John could manage. He was overwhelmed.

"Arn Lindquist, who will be managing the office, has arranged for your family to occupy a lovely town house not far from the office. Your wife will love it. It comes with servants. It should be a great experience for your kids as well."

"I'm flabbergasted," John exclaimed. "It sounds really exciting."

"I wasn't certain exactly when school lets out so you can have your secretary make all the flight arrangements, and make sure your passports are current." Bowers continued. "We have every faith in you, my boy. We know you will do a bang up job." The boss picked up his telephone, signaling that it was John's time to retreat.

John waited until dinner that evening to announce the big news. He breathed a sigh of relief when the entire family was genuinely excited about the trip. Brett could not wait to tell his friends.

"Can we take Mai with us?" Tiffany asked. Mai Ling was the Smith's pure bred Shih Tzu. She was a nervous and edgy female, and John was sure she had been inbred at some puppy mill.

"No darling," Jane said. "I think I'll hire a dog and a house sitter, who can take care of Mai, and make sure that the house stays clean and safe. It would be an ideal job for a college student who is home for the summer. I wonder if the Dawson boy would be interested."

Jake Dawson was a student at The University of Florida in Gainesville. The Smiths were very friendly with his parents who lived about a mile away. They belonged to the same country club. At the university Jake roomed with a young lad from Florida's panhandle. Billy was quite poor, and he was attending the school on a scholarship. His parents and siblings were real crackers. He was two years older than Jake. After high school he got certified as a massage therapist, and he had begun to earn some money at that trade, but when his scholarship came through, it was his opportunity to get out of the sticks.

He often told Jake that he hated the thought of going home for the summer. He lived in a trailer with his parents, two younger sisters and his maternal grandfather. The adults all smoked and he couldn't tolerate it. To make matters worse they guzzled a case of beer almost every evening. In fact he admitted that he never wanted to go home again. Jake felt really bad for him, but when he asked his parents if Billy could come home with him for the summer, he got a resounding, "No!!"

Jake's parents gave Jane Smith his telephone number, and when she called about the house sitting job, he agreed immediately to take it on. Now Billy could come home with him for the summer. They could both stay at the Smith house and nobody need know of Billy's existence. He saw no problem in putting up a quiet boy like Billy in a five bedroom house. He knew enough hot females to fix them both up all summer. Billy accepted the invitation at once, and breathed a sigh of relief that he didn't have to go back to the trailer and his obnoxious family.

Billy had another reason for appreciating his good fortune. He was madly in love with Jake. He knew that Jake was straight and he never made a move on him or let on to anyone at school that he was gay. He even double dated with Jake, but avoided sex if he could. If he couldn't avoid it, he just pretended that he was fucking Jake and somehow he managed to please the young co-ed he was with. Jake had no idea of Billy's true feelings.

When Jake made him the offer to come home with him for the summer, Billy jumped at the chance. He hoped that if he was alone in a big house with Jake for several weeks, things might happen. He grew excited at the prospect. He couldn't wait to drive north in Jake's sporty car. He had never been out of Florida his entire life.

Jake arrived in Hewlett Harbor, Long Island on the morning of the Smith's departure. He dropped Billy off at a local ice cream store and told him to wait there. He had arranged to drive the Smiths to the airport in their big Mercedes and then he would come back for Billy. After he dropped Billy off, he made a quick stop at home to say hello to his parents. Then he drove to the Smiths.

Billy sat at a table nursing a coke when three young men, obviously college students, came into the shop. They were all just shy of six feet tall. One of them was blond, one had a strong square chin and the third was built like a brick shithouse. Billy stared at them and his cock began to rise. If anything turned Billy on, it was blond hair, a square chin and a muscular body, and there were all three elements right in front of him. The three youths bought ice cream cones and went on their way. They didn't even see Billy sitting in the corner, and Billy did nothing to draw attention to himself.

Jake had three suitcases, and John helped him to the guest bedroom. One of the suitcases was Billy's. There were actually two guest bedrooms in the house. One was intended as a maid's room. Jake thought that Billy could sleep there. He had to hang out with the Smiths for more than an hour as it was too early to go to JFK. During that time, Jane gave him full instructions, mostly about feeding and walking Mai. All Jake could think about was Billy hanging out all alone at the ice cream parlor, in a strange place, where people spoke in New York accents that he might not even understand. Jake could barely understand Billy's exaggerated southern drawl. Actually, Billy was doing just fine admiring the eye candy coming into the ice cream shop.

Jake sent the Smiths off with full assurance that they didn't have to worry about a thing. He rushed back to town, picked up Billy, and the boys got themselves settled in the house. For no explainable reason at all, Mai kept yelping at Jake. She wouldn't let him near her, but she jumped into Billy's lap and rubbed her nose on his hand. Billy stroked her tummy, and he instantly had a new friend.

"You can take care of the bitch," Jake observed.

"Sure thing," Billy said as he hugged Mai.

The boys double dated two or three nights a week. Jake paid for everything. This disturbed Billy a great deal, but there wasn't much he could do about it. There was no way he could even dream of reciprocating. Ironically, Billy was actually more successful with the girls than Jake was. The local women adored his southern accent. His good looks helped a lot also. Billy was 6'2" and all muscle. He had blond hair, blue eyes and word got around that he had 8 glorious inches of hard, uncut cock. His body was smooth and hairless. His lips were full and sensuous. At first glance it looked like he might be wearing lipstick. His chin was square and he had a tiny cleft in it.

Jake wasn't bad looking either, but the boys were quite different. Jake was swarthy looking. He stood 5'11" tall. He too was muscular. His hair was black and curly. His eyes were dark brown and very inviting. He had a button nose, which gave him a boyish look. His chest was hairy and he had a line of fine hair running from his chest right down to his pubes. He was cut, and about six and a half inches erect. Word got around that he was a gifted and satisfying lover. Billy, of course, yearned to find that out for himself. He continued to fantasize that he was with Jake whenever he was with a woman.

Jake didn't dare take Billy to his country club to swim or eat. He was afraid that his parents would learn of his existence and disapprove. They spent their afternoons sun bathing nude on the patio. Billy was surprised that the daily temperatures were just as high in Long Island as they were in Florida this time of year, but the humidity was considerably lower, and so the heat was much more bearable.

In Stockholm, Jane and the kids rarely saw John. He was putting in fifteen to seventeen hour days, so they spent their days sightseeing and swimming. Jane was particularly enjoying having a maid do all the housework, and the cooking as well. The kids didn't particularly like all the fish in the Scandinavian diet, but they didn't complain. They even made some friends on the street where they lived. Everyone they met spoke English to some degree, and they tried to return the favor by learning some Swedish. It was indeed a unique opportunity for all of them.

One of Brett's new friends was Sven Lindquist, the son of Arn Lindquist. The Lindquists rented the town house two doors down from the Smiths. Arn was a widower, and Sven was his only child. Sven's mother died tragically of ovarian cancer when he was a toddler. Arn never remarried. Instead, he threw himself into his work, leaving Sven to be raised mostly by nannies.

Two weeks into the trip, John got a call from Mr. Franklin at the home office.

"John," he sounded frantic. "Thank goodness I got hold of you. Listen. Ralph has royally fucked up some of your accounts. We've had lots of complaints. You've got to come home for a week or two, and straighten things out. Hopefully you can train Tim Petty quickly. He's the most promising guy in the office. I hate to ask you to split yourself in half, but I have to."

What could John say? "I'll be on the next plane home, boss, and I'll get into the office as soon as I get over the jet lag."

"You're a saint, John. Safe flight. I can't wait to see you."

Jane and the kids weren't particularly happy to be left alone in Stockholm for two or three weeks, but since they hardly saw John anyway, they didn't complain.

When John arrived at JFK, he thought of calling Jake, but then he decided that he would surprise him. Also, he reasoned that if he took a cab, he could get home sooner. Every bone in his body ached from the long trip, and he needed sleep badly.

He let himself into the house with his house key, but didn't see anyone. Usually Mai barked her dislike for him, but even she was silent. He thought Jake might be out on the patio with Mai so he headed that way. He was right. Jake was sunning himself on a lounge and next to him, on another lounge, was the handsomest young man John had ever seen. Mai was curled up on the guy's lap. Jake and the stranger were both naked. John could not help himself. He gawked at Billy's ample package, which was on display.

John opened the patio door noisily, so as to give them some warning. There was no way either man could grab a robe because they hadn't brought one out with them. They both jumped up and poor Mai got dumped on the concrete slab. Both of them tried to hide their packages, but it was a losing battle. John started to laugh.

"Carry on men," he said. "I've seen it all before." The two naked specimens laughed and loosened up somewhat.

"I feel a little overdressed," John stated seriously.

"Gee, I am sorry, sir," Jake said. "I sure as hell didn't expect to see you until the end of August or the beginning of September." John sat down on a chair facing the two boys who had resumed their places on the lounges. As succinctly as he could, he explained his situation and said that he would only be home for a couple of weeks. He also told Jake that he wanted him to stay, and look after the house and dog as they had agreed, because he would be working long hours. When he was through, he added, "Aren't you going to introduce me to your friend?"

"I'm sorry, sir," Jake started, but John interrupted him.

"Please," he said, "call me John. Sir makes me feel like an old man."

"Of course, John," Jake went on. "This is Billy Johnson. He's my room mate at school. He's keeping me company for the summer, and I gave him the maid's room. I hope it's OK with you."

"Sure it is. It's good you have company. I see Mai likes him. That bitch hates me."

"She hates me too," Jake said. "For that reason alone I'm glad Billy is here."

Billy couldn't say a word. He stood there being dumb and numb. Standing in front of him was his vision of the ideal lover. John was tall, blond, blue eyed, square chinned, muscular and drop dead gorgeous. Billy could only imagine what his cock would look like. Fat chance he would ever find out.

"OUCH!" John suddenly yelled out.

"What's wrong?" Billy asked.

"Hell, I'm as stiff as a board from the cramped conditions on that plane, and the extra long trip. Also I'm so tired I can hardly keep my eyes open, so if you guys don't mind, I'm going up to my room and get some shut eye before I have to get back to work tomorrow morning."

"John," Billy said, "I'm a licensed massage therapist. Why don't you let me give you a nice soothing rub down before you go to sleep? It will help get rid of your stiffness and you'll sleep better."

"Wow, that sounds like a great idea. I wanted to get a Swedish massage in Stockholm, but I never had the time. Come on up to my bedroom and we'll do it," John grinned at Billy. That grin and John's double entendre melted Billy's heart. He instantly transferred his unfulfilled lust from Jake to John.

"Go ahead," Jake said. I have to go down to the store and get some extra stuff since there will be three for dinner. When I get back, I'll start the meal going so take your time Billy, and do a real good job." Jake ran off to his room to dress.

"I need to get some stuff from my room," Billy told John. "You go to your bedroom and strip to your underwear. Lie on your stomach and I'll be there shortly."

John smiled at Billy, picked up his two suitcases from where he left them in the front hall, and proceeded up the stairs. He left his door open so Billy went right in a few minutes later. He had put on a pair of tight gym shorts which hardly hid his ripped body, and certainly did not hide his package. He carried a case similar to a doctor's bag, which he placed on the dresser. He removed some sort of lotion and a hand towel from the bag.

John was already laying on his stomach in his king size bed. He was clad only in a pair of boxer shorts. The shorts were tapered and were slit on the sides. They barely covered more than what a pair of jockey shorts would have. Billy stopped for a moment to admire John's lean and muscular backside. He was about 6 feet tall and lacked body fat. Obviously John worked out a lot. His hair was blond and had a decided wave. Billy couldn't wait to see the rest of John. He knew he had blue eyes, a square chin and needed a shave. He couldn't wait to see the man's cock and balls. Billy's lust was turning to a burning desire, but he knew he needed to control himself. He was grateful that John had his eyes closed and couldn't see his rising cock. He needn't have worried. John was more asleep than awake.

Billy climbed on the bed and straddled John. He was on his knees, which were on either side of John's thighs. For a brief second, Billy had a vision of entering John doggy style, but he forced the thought out of his head. Instead he poured some lotion in the palm of his hand, put the bottle down on the bedside table, and began to massage John's shoulders. His strong hands kneaded John's shoulders, digging in deeply and satisfyingly.

John began to purr like a baby as Billy squeezed his shoulders. After a while, Billy started descending down John's backside. He kneaded every muscle he could reach down to the shorts. Then he did John's thighs, calves, and each toe individually. When he kneaded the underside of John's feet, John began to twitch and giggle in his sleep. Billy realized that John was very ticklish on the soles of his feet. He would have liked to have stretched John's legs and arms, as he usually did, but he was afraid he would wake him up. He asked John to turn over, but he was fast asleep and didn't move. Billy grew bold. He hooked his fingers in the waistband of John's shorts and gingerly pulled them down and removed them. He poured fresh lotion on his hands and started to caress John's bubbly ass.

"Aah," he heard John mutter in his sleep. Billy figured that if John woke up and berated him for pulling down his shorts he could always say it was done as part of the full body massage he was giving him. Billy grew bolder and started to rub up and down John's crack.

He felt John tense, but he didn't wake up. John's lips simply said, "Mmmmmmm..." He was obviously enjoying the massage. Billy wondered if he could turn him over and get to do his front. He decided to try. If John awoke, he would give him the choice of continuing the massage or going back to sleep.

Billy shook John's shoulder. "Turn over," he said softly. To his delight John turned over on his back. He awakened for a second, but went right back to sleep. Billy was awestruck. John had an erection. He was uncircumcised and at least eight inches standing straight up in the air. His cock was rather wide around also. Billy hesitated. How was he going to avoid touching that beautiful monster?

He moistened his palms again and massaged John's legs first. Then he started working on his chest. He was gentle, very gentle. John continued to sleep peacefully. Billy started working on John's abdomen, and marveled at how hard it was. John still continued to sleep.

Finally lust overtook reason and Billy wrapped his hand around John's cock. He was surprised that the head was covered with precum, which now blended with the ointment. John heaved a loud sigh, but continued sleeping. He was snoring lightly. Billy continued to stroke John's cock lightly. He fondled John's balls as he continued to stroke. He felt John's balls constricting and realized that he was about to cum. Billy didn't want to mess up the bed so without thinking he simply went down on John and sucked him until John was drained out.

Billy was totally unaware of it, but when he went down on John, John put his hand on Billy's head and urged his cock deeper into Billy's mouth. Sometime during the last seconds, John had awakened. He realized what was happening, and absolutely allowed it. Billy did not release John's cock until he sucked it dry. Now he panicked. What could he do but beat a hasty retreat. When he started to get off the bed, John said, "Please don't go. Lie here beside me."

Billy was shocked, but pleased, and did as John asked. As they lay side by side, John reached under the waist band of Billy's gym shorts and caressed his waiting cock. "Take them off," John whispered in Billy's ear. Billy removed his shorts, and John started stroking the prize in his hand. Billy was almost there even before John took him in hand. John sensed it and went down on Billy. Billy was surprised at how expertly John was sucking his cock. *He's no amateur,* Billy thought as he gave way to a mind blowing orgasm. John swallowed every drop, and then kissed Billy with his mouth open so that they could share the residue.

They lay hunkered together, fondling each other until they heard Jake return. Billy jumped out of bed, put on his shorts, gathered his lotions, towels and bag, and ran downstairs to the maid's room.

Not a word had been spoken about what had occurred between them, but lady luck was smiling. At dinner, Jake announced that he had to drive his kid sister up to sleep away summer camp the next day, and would be gone over night. She had missed the camp bus, and the first few days of camp, because she had been suffering from a very bad cold. He asked Billy to please cover for him.

"My pleasure," Billy said enthusiastically. "After all you've done for me, it's the least that I can do."

After dinner, John excused himself. "I'm off to bed," he said. "I'm not over jet lag." Jake and Billy cleaned up, and then Jake said that he needed to turn in early also. He said he would be out of the house before six the next morning. Billy then went to his room and watched television. He couldn't get over John's reaction, and his surprising response to his impulsive acts of love. It was obvious that John wanted more, and they would be alone in the house the next evening.

Early the next morning, Jake was gone before Billy even woke up. It was barely dawn when Billy's door opened silently and John walked in completely naked. He got into bed, and hunkered up to Billy. He twisted around into a sixty-nine position, and of course that totally woke up the sleeping guest. It took about a second for him to assess the situation before his mouth gobbled up John's dick which was wet with precum. The two men came so close in time, you could say it was simultaneous. When they were both flaccid again, John twisted around so that they were lying facing each other with their cocks rubbing together.

At last John spoke. "That was fantastic," he announced. He jumped out of bed. "I have to get ready for work. I'll try to get home as early as possible, and I promise we'll have a blast. Don't worry about breakfast. I'll grab something in The City. By the way, please try to talk more when my cock's not in your mouth. Your accent turns me on and makes me so horny I cannot describe the things I think of doing to you." He was gone and out of the house in less than forty-five minutes, while Billy just lounged contentedly in bed.

John took the railroad to Manhattan. He was basking in a euphoric afterglow, and his mind wandered back to other times and other places.

He remembered that it was just past his fourteenth birthday. He got a summer job with Demetrius, the landscaper. Demetrius worked alone, but he needed a gofer and a laborer to help him with the gardening chores. He was a short man, no more than five feet five inches, but he was stocky and all muscle. His shirt was always open and he displayed a rather hairy chest. John reckoned that Demetrius was pushing forty. Even so, he was completely bald.

At the end of the very first day Demetrius said to John, "My friend, you are filthy, and your clothes are a mess. Tomorrow bring a change of clothes, but for today, you'll come home with me and I'll clean you up and give you something of mine to wear home. It will be big on you, but you will manage."

When they got to Demetrius' home, Demetrius took John into a shed behind the house. "There's a shower in here," he said. "This way, I never have to go into the house as dirty as we are. I keep some clothes in here to change into. It's too bad the shed isn't attached to the house so I could enter in my birthday suit." Somehow that struck him funny, and Demetrius broke out into a gale of laughter.

Immediately after they stepped into the shed, Demetrius undressed so rapidly that John could only stare. What he stared at was Demetrius' engorged and very erect seven inch uncut cock. "Come on boy," he said. "We haven't got all day. Get undressed. I gotta get you home." John got undressed as quickly as possible and stepped into the shower with his boss. Demetrius was already soaped up and he handed the bar to John.

After John soaped himself up and watched the water flush his dirt down the drain, Demetrius grabbed the soap from him, and turned him around. Demetrius started to soap John's back and buttocks. "When I'm through," he said, "you can do me." John got more than he bargained for. Demetrius soaped John's ass crack and even inserted a finger or two, which made John jump.

"It's nice and clean now," Demetrius said, and he got down on his knees and started to rim John's ass. At the same time he reached around and wrapped John's nearly mature cock in his hand, and started stroking it. John was in disbelief. Things like this happened to other boys, never to him. He was about to shoot a load when Demetrius turned him around again and took John's cock in his mouth. Demetrius' tongue and lips finished the job. He swallowed every drop and announced, "You sure taste good boy. Now what are you going to do for me?" He hugged John tightly, and almost crushed the boy with his big, burly arms. He kissed him full on the lips and John was shocked at how much he enjoyed it.

"I'll do exactly the same to you," John announced with a mile wide smile on his face.

He and Demetrius made love in the shower all summer, every day after work. Demetrius taught John how to fuck him and little by little, with a lot of patience, John took Demetrius' cock into his ass. John would cum once or twice as the big man's cock massaged his prostate. It was at those times that John concluded that ass fucking was the best way ever to have sex. At the end of the summer, before school was to start again, Demetrius asked John if he wanted to work for him again the following summer. John nodded and answered by planting a big wet kiss on Demetrius' lips.

John had three glorious summers with Demetrius. After the third summer, Demetrius was killed in a barroom brawl. The killer told the police that Demetrius had come on to him sexually. When he refused to take no for an answer, he became aggressive and the man said he was forced to kill him. The crime was classified as justifiable homicide and the killer got off Scott free. Ever since then, John had dreamed and fantasized about man with man sex, but he didn't dare to admit that he might be gay, even to himself. He resisted all temptation until years later when he joined a country club while still living in Los Angeles.

Things went well for him and his family. They bought a house in Beverly Hills, and joined The West Los Angeles Country Club. It was at the club that John gave into temptation. Jamie, the bartender was a flamboyant gay man, and very handsome at that. As was the habit of most members, they would enjoy a drink at the bar after a game of golf or tennis. Jamie quickly developed a crush on John and began to flirt with him quite innocently. He never expected John to respond, but respond he did, and it wasn't long before John and Jamie were fucking each other whenever they could.

They had no set schedule, but when John was available, he would wait for Jamie in the parking lot after Jamie's shift. He would follow the bartender home, where he was always pleasantly surprised. Jamie would shower while John waited for him in bed. He would come out of the shower, scrubbed clean, all his makeup removed, and appearing very manly. Their "affair" lasted until Jamie became involved with the stepson of the tennis pro, and one day he told John that he was now monogamous. John returned to his life, full of frustration and constantly yearning for male sex.

But his attitude was different now; no more holding back. He joined a gym and worked out constantly. At the gym he managed to have a few encounters with other men. It wasn't the greatest, but it kept him from going crazy.

So when Billy came on to him and gave him the kind of sex and pleasure that he longed for, he was elated. He even pretended to be asleep, hoping that Billy would get bolder, and he did. All he could think of during the rest of the commute, and all day at work, was having Billy alone with him in the house all night.

As for Billy, he nearly went crazy with anticipation. To keep busy, he cleaned every room in the house, even Jake's messy space. He changed the sheets on John's bed and washed everything dirty in the hamper. He dried and folded everything, and put all the sheets and pillow cases neatly away. When he had no housework left, he raided the refrigerator and the freezer. He found the ingredients for a great dinner for the two of them. He defrosted a tray of shrimp with cocktail sauce, and two filet mignon steaks, which he intended to barbeque on the patio. After they were defrosted he marinated the steaks in garlic salt. He found four sweet potatoes in the pantry and took out two to bake for dinner. In the liquor cabinet he found a few bottles of red wine. He knew nothing about wines, but he took out one that looked expensive and he erroneously refrigerated it.

Finally, he washed the patio table and chairs, found a table cloth to cover the table, and set it with dishes, glasses and utensils for dinner. Still having time left, he showered and dressed in his sexiest garments. He wore no underwear, a pair of cargo shorts and a tank top shirt. He put on a pair of flip flops and went back to the patio. There he sat on a lounge chair, fidgeting, and waiting for John to come home.

John was swamped at work, and he didn't manage to get out as early as he would have liked. Still it was only eight o'clock when he arrived home. Billy awaited him at the front door and he was greeted with a bone crushing hug from John.

"Let's go to bed," John announced.

"Not yet. You have to be patient. I've prepared a great dinner for us. Why don't you go upstairs and shower. I'll have everything ready by the time you return."

John returned wearing nothing but a pair of gym shorts and flip flops. He hugged Billy again. This time they kissed sensuously. The steaks were sizzling on the barbeque and the potatoes were baking in the oven. The shrimp cocktail was on the table and ready to eat. It was a struggle to let go of each other and eat their dinner, but somehow they did. They even took the time to clean up.

"You can't put me off any longer," John said. He took Billy's hand and they rushed up to John's bedroom. They both undressed, taking off what little they had on. They hugged and tongue kissed and rubbed their cocks together. Billy did not tire of rubbing his hands up and down John's hard body. He made a silent resolution to work out more. At last they both fell on the bed.

"Fuck me, please," John begged. "I have waited so long for this." Billy smiled as John handed him a tube of lubricant. They were both rock hard so no preliminaries were necessary. Both Demetrius and Jamie used to fuck John doggy style so he turned on his stomach.

"Please turn on your back," Billy said. "I want to be able to see your face and kiss you while I fuck you." This was a new position for John and he anticipated it eagerly. Both his former lovers had stretched John to his limits, and fortunately he was still wide open. He accepted Billy's cock easily. The moment John's prostate was engaged in the action, he felt his first orgasm building. In fact, he came twice before Billy exploded up his ass. They fucked each other back and forth until the early hours of the morning. John was insatiable and Billy didn't try to discourage him, even when he was dog tired.

Over the next two weeks, the lovers were able to sneak in a few quickies while Jake slept, but the encounters were rare. Billy still had to go out in the evenings with Jake, so that he wouldn't become suspicious. It was killing him that he couldn't be with John. John was equally distressed.

When John had to return to Stockholm, the boys drove him to the airport. Mai slept contentedly in Billy's lap during the entire trip. They shook hands and wished John a safe trip. Billy wanted desperately to embrace John, but he couldn't of course.

Now that Billy's existence was known to the owner of the house, Jake introduced him to his family, and said that Mr. Smith had approved of Billy occupying the maid's room for the summer. At least the boys didn't have to sneak around anymore, and Jake's parents even entertained both of them with dinner, and sometimes lunch, at their country club.

Billy and John never saw each other again. For the remainder of his time in school, Billy worked part time in a fitness center. It was an excellent environment for him to meet other gay men. Needless to say, he was very popular, and he finally came out to Jake. Jake could not believe it. After all, he was aware of how well Billy did with the ladies. Nevertheless, they continued to be friends and room mates. Jake went home for the summers without Billy, who worked all summer at the fitness center.

Although they remained good friends, after graduation they lost touch with each other. Billy never returned to his trailer home. He got a good job with an investment company in Miami. He had given some thought to trying to get a job in New York with John's firm, but he decided that it would not be wise. John was married and in the closet, and he thought it best to leave it that way. In Miami he met another young man, Marc Wyman. It wasn't long before they moved in together and committed to a life partnership.

Billy constantly wondered if John could return to his wife, and his marital status, without yearning for him and for other men. Of course, he would never contact him, and so he would never know if John ever had sex again with another man. If John wanted to remain in the closet, it was his choice. If he wanted to live a double life, it was his choice also.

The plain truth was that John spent most of his time in Sweden working with Arn Lindquist. They sometimes endured long and arduous hours at the new branch office. One night they had dinner together and drank too much. When they got back to the office, which was empty except for them, one thing led to another, and John enjoyed gay sex with a very oversexed Swede. They continued the relationship for the rest of John's stay in Sweden.

Billy always looked back on his brief encounter with John Smith as the best and shortest summer romance anybody ever had. John felt the same way about Billy and Arn.

PART TWO

When John returned to Stockholm, he was miserable and frustrated. He spent more and more time at the office to avoid having sex with Jane. He urged Arn to go home at a decent hour, but Arn chose to remain in the office. They spent many long hours alone in the empty office. The two men took a little time off every evening to have a quick dinner and relax. It was the only down time they allowed.

It was at these informal dinners that they learned more and more about each other. They found themselves opening up and baring secrets that they never thought they would tell another human being. Arn admitted that he hadn't ever been that much in love with his wife. He got drunk one night at a party and she seduced him by going down on him. When he was hard and beyond the point of no return, she made him enter her. The result was Sven, and a shotgun wedding. He was sad when she developed ovarian cancer and died a couple of years later, but he loved raising Sven all by himself in an all male household.

This prompted John to admit that he was attracted to Jane, and she put out, so he figured what the hell, and they got married, but he never really loved her in the classic sense. It was never a great love affair. Arn had admitted that he preferred to be in an all male environment, so John wondered if he should tell Arn about Demetrius and Jamie or about his escapades at the fitness center, but he held back.

One evening over dinner, he asked Arn if he had ever loved another woman, since he never really loved his wife. "No," Arn said, "how about you?"

"Not ever," John answered.

They went back to the office and John mentioned that his back was killing him. Arn said that he gave a great massage, and urged John to remove his shirt and lie down on the reception room couch. Without thinking, John began to laugh and said, "When I went home for those two weeks, I got a massage with relief."

"Was she a good looking masseuse, or a bull dyke?" Arn asked.

"*HE* was a handsome young college student," John answered, and immediately regretted saying it. He didn't know why he said it, and he didn't know what to say now, so he simply shut up.

The silence was forever, until Arn said, "Loosen your belt and pull down your pants a little so I can get to the small of your back."

"We better stop now," John said kindly. "That's how it started with the college student."

Then John got the shock of his life. "That's exactly what I had in mind," Arn said.

It was Arn who picked the Smith family up at the airport in a seven seater mini van. He knew that Brett Smith was the same age as his son, and he insisted that Sven go with him to the airport. Sven objected vehemently, but in the end he went along for the ride.

Fortunately the two boys hit it off immediately. Sven introduced Brett to other boys on their street, and soon he was playing soccer (futball) with them almost every day. His mother and sister went shopping all the time, and Brett was happy to be relieved of such nonsense. The Lindquist's housekeeper and cook left every day after she made sure that Sven had a good supper. Arn was rarely home before nine in the evening. Jane often had Sven for dinner and he would spend the evening until she shooed him home and off to bed. If Sven ate at home, Brett would go to the Lindquists after dinner and keep his friend company until it was time for bed.

On the evening that Arn gave John the first of many massages, Brett went over to Sven's house after dinner. The two boys were

playing video games in Sven's bedroom, when Arn called. He told
Sven that he would be particularly late that night, and if Sven was
uncomfortable being alone he should sleep over at the Smiths. Shortly
after that Jane called, and told Sven to pack his sleepwear and come
over to spend the night as both fathers would be very late getting
home. Brett had a big double bed, and the boys agreed it would be
fun to share it.

Jane made them get into bed at about 9:30 PM. She shut the
bedroom light and as she closed the door she said, "You two better
go right to sleep. No fooling around, you hear?" As soon as the door
was closed, Sven asked, "Do you want to jerk off together?"

"I was afraid to ask you" Brett said. He had been doing it
pretty regularly, but he was ashamed to let Sven know, thinking Sven
might consider it to be dirty and taboo.

Sven expressed surprise, and said, "It's the greatest feeling in
the world. Why would you be shy about asking me?"

"I honestly don't know why."

"OK, get naked," Sven said, and he removed his PJ bottoms,
which was all he had put on. Brett did the same. Brett expected
Sven to start stroking himself, but Sven had other things in mind. He
wrapped his hand around Brett's maturing cock and began stroking.
Brett was shocked, but made no move to stop Sven. This just felt
too good. He got hard pretty quickly, and he began to feel an orgasm
coming on.

Sven could sense that Brett was near. "Doesn't it feel great?"
he asked.

"Yes, oh yes," Brett said breathlessly. "Please don't stop."

"I didn't intend to," Sven said. Then he did something Brett
was totally unprepared for. He bent over, took Brett's cock in his
mouth and began to stroke it with his tongue. Brett immediately had
an orgasm. Sven swallowed all Brett's cum and declared that it was
delicious.

The two boys lay still for a few minutes and Sven said, "Just
before last Christmas, I was searching through my dad's closet to see
if I could find where he hid my gifts. On the top shelf, way at the
back, I found a DVD with two naked men on the cover. One of them

had the other's pecker in his mouth. I played the DVD and wow did I learn a lot. Tomorrow when our fathers go to work, would you like to see it?"

"Yes," Brett said eagerly. "Now can I do it to you?"

"Do what?"

"What you just did to me," Brett giggled. He took hold of Sven's cock gently and started stroking. As soon as he felt Sven's hardness, Brett leaned over and started sucking as Sven had. Sven's cock head was full of pre-cum and Brett sucked it up eagerly. It didn't take long for Sven to reach nirvana. He muffled his screeches as best he could, and Brett swallowed as much of Sven's cum as he could.

Afterwards they lay naked, side by side, and Sven took hold of Brett's hand. He leaned over and kissed Brett gently on his lips. There was no tongue action involved.

"I love you, you know," Sven said to the amazed Brett.

Brett remained silent. His brain was working overtime. Finally he said, "Geeze Sven, I love you too. I never want to go home. What are we going to do?"

At about that time, their two fathers finally admitted to each other what they both had been longing for, and they had stripped naked. Arn was completing John's massage in the manner he had desired. He was down on his colleague sucking him as sensuously as he could. John returned the favor a little bit later. Afterward they lay on the couch crushed together, kissing desperately, as if it was the last kiss each would ever have. Their tongues were dueling, and they were both moaning as their cocks rubbed together.

Finally Arn mumbled in John's ear. "I've wanted this since the minute I laid eyes on you at the airport. I trust you enough to tell you that I have been gay all my life. That one time with my wife was an anomaly. I don't regret it, however, because I have Sven, and I keep my secret because of him. I have led a pretty celibate life since Maria died. I don't want him to know that his old man is a fag."

"I don't like that word," John admonished Arn. "Let me tell you that I have been gay, or at least I realized that I was gay since I was fourteen." He then told Arn about Demetrius and decided to leave Jamie for another time. I married because Jane could arouse me and I didn't want to lead a gay life. At least that was true until now. I love you Arn and this is quite a dilemma we have created."

"I know," Arn said. "Let's not think of it for now. Let's just have fun. Tomorrow, I'll bring lubricant with me, if you would like that."

"I'd love that," John answered as he resumed kissing Arn.

The remaining few weeks of the Smith's stay in Stockholm passed all too quickly. John had to resign himself to the fact that it was time to go home. School was starting in less than a week. He made up an excuse that he needed just a few more days and he sent his family home ahead of him. He had to give up the rented house and he stayed with Arn, but occupied the guest room. At night he would steal into Arn's bedroom and the two men would make love all night. John would sneak out to his room before Sven woke up, attempting to keep his and Arn's love a secret.

Finally he ran out of excuses to stay, and arranged for a flight home. On his last night in Sweden, he and Arn "had to work late" at the office. They coupled for the last time, each crying his eyes out, not knowing how they would survive without the other.

In the four years that followed, John and Arn, Brett and Sven stayed in close contact via E Mails, text messages and telephone calls. Absence did indeed make their hearts grow fonder and their yearnings greater.

During the past year both Bowers and Franklin retired and John was made CEO of the firm. One of the first things he did was to arrange for a two week managers' conference at corporate headquarters in New York. He arranged for the meeting to be in the summer. Some of the managers had young children and John encouraged them to bring their families along. When he knew who was coming alone, and who was coming with families, he arranged for the appropriate amount of rooms at a fine New York hotel.

John lied to Jane and told her that he would stay in The City during the meeting days at the same hotel, because the training sessions would be long and arduous. He also told her that the seminar would last for three weeks. He had previously talked Arn into staying an extra week. After thinking about it for awhile, Jane announced that during that time she would take her daughter and go back to Los Angeles to visit her aging parents. John was thrilled and Brett was ecstatic. Brett told John that he and Sven would stay at the house during those three weeks while he and Arn were at the hotel.

John and Brett met their lovers at the airport. None of them gave any hints as to their true feelings and shook hands cordially. John and Arn took a limo to the hotel and Brett drove Sven to his now empty home. They didn't even wait to get to a bedroom but began stripping in the front hall. They stood naked, facing each other, examining their bodies, assessing how much each had changed. They certainly had changed, now that they were each in their eighteenth year. The two men were remarkably alike and could almost have passed for brothers.

Sven was 6'2" tall, lean and muscular, platinum blond hair, blue eyes, very little body hair, a five inch uncut cock that was currently at full mast and eight inches of hard manhood. Brett was 6'1" tall, muscular but with a few extra attractive pounds, sandy blond hair, blue eyes (but deeper than Sven's), some fuzzy body hair and wonder of wonders, their uncut pricks were identical in size and shape.

After viewing and adoring what they saw, they fell into each other's arms. Their mouths parted and their tongues met. Their cocks ground together and they rubbed against each other. Brett had to pull away because he began to cum. They ran up to Brett's bedroom, and never left, except to pee and eat, for the next two days.

When the next semester was to begin, Brett would be a full time student at Columbia University and would be living on campus. After they had their first orgasms, Sven said, "Brett, my love, I have some fantastic news. My father is letting me finish my education in New York. I am going to Columbia next semester. We must go to the school housing as soon as possible, and arrange to room together."

Brett gave out a screech and almost crushed Sven's bones.

"I won't be going home with my father. Do you think your folks would let me stay here until school starts?"

"Jerk, of course they will."

John arranged for adjoining rooms at the hotel. It would be unseemly for him and Arn to room together. As soon as they entered their rooms, they opened the adjoining door. John rushed into Arn's room and they began to kiss as ardently as their sons had. As they kissed they stripped. When they were naked they stood admiring each other appreciatively.

They were in their early forties now, but they both had bodies of steel from their long work outs in their gyms. They were both 6' tall, blond hair, blue eyes, virtually hairless, and they possessed the same size uncut cocks. After staring at John's cock for a moment, Arn fell to his knees and started sucking it. That began a full day and night of sucking and fucking. They took a moment to call the boys who assured them that they were doing fine.

John and Arn managed somehow to concentrate on the seminars. They had their meals with their fellow managers, but always claimed to be tired, and they would slip off early to their respective rooms. The others couldn't even talk them into taking in a Broadway show.

At last the two weeks ended. The managers went home, all except Arn. He packed and he and John rented a limo and started off to Hewlett Harbor. John continued his lie. He told the boys that the seminar went so well, it was cut short by a week and the Lindquists were staying on for the third week as guests in the Smith house.

Brett and Sven had been talking for many long hours before their dad's were due to arrive home. They did a lot of soul searching. They didn't want to sleep in separate rooms for the rest of Sven's stay, so they decided to come out to their fathers and to Jane, when she returned in a couple of weeks.

Arn and John did not have that luxury. Arn would have to occupy the guest room and they would manage as best they could until Arn returned to Stockholm. As soon as their fathers were settled in their rooms, and they were all getting ready to go to the country club for dinner, the boys said they needed to talk. Actually Brett did the talking. He explained to the older men that he and Sven had been committed to each other since the summer they met in Stockholm. They went on to ask permission to sleep together while they were under John's roof.

The fathers were speechless and very envious. Finally John spoke. "We love you both," he said, "that will never change, so be happy and live your lives the way you want to and not how others want you to." Arn started to cry and he and Sven embraced.

"I am so happy for you," Arn said

"Well," John said, "let's go to the club and celebrate." Then he embraced his son as Arn had embraced his, and they both had a good cry.

They met Jake Dawson and his lovely bride at the club. John asked Jake if he ever heard from Billy, and Jake just shook his head sadly. John was sad too. He would have welcomed some news about the young man, who had given him such a delightful summer romance. He wondered if he should try to locate him and contact him, but promptly put that thought out of his head.

Brett's room adjoined John and Jane's. Since Brett had never entertained in his room until now, John was unaware that you could hear everything that went on in either room. As a child Brett used to hear his parents making love, and when he got older, he jerked off to their moans and groans. Ever since the Stockholm trip, he hardly heard them anymore.

That night when they all retired, Brett and Sven discreetly closed their door. When they started to make love, John was shocked. He could hear every sigh, moan and groan. Even their muffled cries at climax were clear to him. He was so aroused he could barely breathe.

Arn waited until he believed the boys would be asleep. He crept into John's room, closing the door securely behind him. What he did not know was that the two young men were wide awake. They had each just had great orgasms and were now basking in the afterglow.

When Arn crept into his bed, John was about to tell him that maybe they should go to the guest room, but suddenly some devil in him took over. Perversely he wanted the boys to know about his relationship with Arn. He could not imagine why. He could not fathom the consequences, or if there would even be any, but he was tired of living a lie. He wouldn't be hurting Arn. After all Arn had no wife. It would certainly be easier for him to let the boys hear the love making, than for him to tell them verbally that their fathers were fucking each other. Anyway he doubted he had the courage to tell them. He wasn't sure if the boys were awake or asleep, but he started to make love to Arn and he was very noisy. Subconsciously that encouraged Arn to let loose in the noise department as well. Arn didn't know yet that their sons could hear every sound in the room next door.

Sven was the first to speak after the love noises began. "What's that?" he asked nobody in particular.

"Oh my God," Brett explained. "My mother must have come home early. They're making love."

"I never heard anyone come in after we went to bed," Sven said.

FUCK ME HARDER they heard a voice exclaim.

"Hell and damnation," Sven said. "That's my father. Our fathers are going at it. What are we going to do?"

"Nothing!" Brett said. "They must know, or at least my father must know, that we can hear them. I've heard my dad make love many times through these walls, and he has never been this noisy. You know what I think? I think they want us to know about them. That's what I think."

"I won't be able to face them in the morning."

"Why not?" Brett asked.

"Your father has a wife. Technically he's cheating, and he wants his own son to know. That's pretty perverse, don't you think?"

"Whatever it is, we're not telling my mother. The question is do we tell our fathers that we know?" Just then John gave out a blood curdling scream as he exploded in Arn's ass.

"If they don't know we know after that, then they are both deaf and dumb," Brett said.

Everyone was strangely quiet at breakfast the next morning. It was Saturday and the fathers had the next two days at home. Finally Brett could stand it no longer.

"Don't you two guys have something you would like to share with us?" he asked.

After some hesitation, Arn and John answered simultaneously, "No! Nothing I can think of."

More hesitation, and then Sven said, "I hope we didn't make too much noise last night, John. I just realized that our bedroom is next to yours."

"Actually," John said, "I could hear every sound. It was quite arousing."

"I'm sorry I didn't get to hear all that stuff," Arn said.

Sven was speechless, but Brett couldn't take it any longer. "Look," he said, "we could hear you two guys going at it last night. Now we don't want to judge, but what gives? You didn't try to hide it last night, so why are you denying it this morning?"

The two fathers looked at each other and finally Arn said, "OK, I'll go first."

He explained how he had been gay all his life, but once and only once, Sven's mother seduced him and Sven was conceived. They got married, and Arn tried to have sex with his wife, but he mostly failed. She didn't seem to mind, and they found out later it was because she was suffering from ovarian cancer. "I stayed practically celibate all these years so as not to hurt you," Arn explained to Sven, "but in the end I could not help falling in love with John." There were tears in his eyes. Sven wrapped his arms around his father, and they kissed on the lips.

"Well," Sven said. "It's more usual for a son to come out to his father. This is quite a reversal, and I might add, a very pleasant one." Now all eyes turned to John who recounted his whole history. This time he included the story of Jamie and his one night stands at the gym.

He looked at Brett. "It's confession time, son," he said. Since I met Arn and we returned from Stockholm, I can count on one hand the number of times your mom and I have had sex."

"I know," Brett said quietly.

"What do you mean you know? How do you know?" John asked his son.

"I used to hear you making love all the time, and I practically never heard you since Stockholm. Dad, you aren't being fair to mom. She deserves a man who will really be into her."

"What are you suggesting?" John asked.

"Divorce, of course."

John began to laugh, but the laugh was bitter. "Arn and I have been making plans for the past four years, and finally everything is falling into place. Arn just received news that his and Sven's green cards are being issued. They will have permanent alien resident status until such time as they apply for citizenship, if they so wish."

Brett couldn't contain himself. He jumped up and embraced Sven, then Arn, and then his father.

"Now that I've been promoted to CEO," John continued, "I need a manager in the New York office to take my place. I've offered Arn the job and he's accepted."

"That's wonderful," Brett said. "Congratulations!"

"Yes," John said, "everything is wonderful except now I have to tell your mother I want a divorce, and the reason I want it. I hope she'll be understanding. I'm so scared."

As it turned out, sex is a greater motivator than the need for comfort and convenience. Jane admitted that she was tired of living like a nun and she had been involved in several affairs in the last four years. She wanted a divorce also, but it was costly to John. She got the house, mortgage free, heavy child support for Tiffany, even greater alimony, a goodly chunk of their investments, and membership in the country club as long as she remained single. John gave it to her gladly.

He and Arn rented a luxury three bedroom penthouse apartment on the upper east side of Manhattan. After the first semester the boys moved out of school housing and into the apartment, which was only minutes from campus. Apparently the apartment had thicker walls than Jane's house, because the two couples rarely heard each other making love.

And they made love often and passionately. The specter of losing the other's love at the end of the summer was a thing of the past. The fleeting nature of summer romances had been replaced by permanent and enduring love.

Author's Note: Suburban New Yorkers refer to Manhattan as The City *when speaking of that magical place. Hence, the several references to* The City *in the story. Hewlett Harbor is a very upscale wealthy suburb of New York City.*

Tale Five: Daughter Monster

PART ONE

Who hasn't heard the story a million times? An angel of a woman consistently falls for the wrong guy, and ruins her life. But I'm sure you have never heard about a greedy, ungrateful, egotistical, femme fatale who falls for Mr. Right and never appreciates what she has. She demands that he spend fortunes on her, take her on extravagant trips, run up big debt on her behalf, and still worship the ground she walks on. I sure never heard that story, until I realized that was my own daughter's Modus Operandi.

The men in her life were generally great guys, all somewhat older than she, with good jobs and no really bad habits, like drugs and booze. But they were in and out of her life before I could even get to know them. Her constant demands for their time, attention and money drove them away rather quickly.

I suppose that I must take the blame for her promiscuous and selfish behavior. I made her that way. Constance was conceived while I was a freshman in college. I thought that I would have to quit school, but a series of fortunate events occurred and I was able to continue my education. First of all, my girlfriend Maureen refused to marry me and she would not think of an abortion. She told me that she would put the child up for adoption. I was opposed to adopting out my child when it had two perfectly healthy parents, and at least one loving parent.

Maureen got ballistic on me. There was no way she would allow her life to be ruined by an unwanted child. Bull crap, I wanted the baby and I got her to surrender her parental rights and give me full custody of our unborn infant.

My parents had always wanted more children after me, but they were unable to conceive another. They were thrilled to take over rearing Connie, and they insisted that I remain in school to continue my education in communications. By the time Connie was six I was a college graduate, had a good job, and I bought a small bungalow just around the corner from my parents where Connie and I took up residence.

I wanted to put Connie in After Care, but my mother wouldn't hear of it. She firmly believed that she had made a million mistakes raising me and she was going to do right by Connie. As a result she became a prison warden in Connie's eyes. Every night when I got home from work Connie met me at the door, crying and complaining about Grandma. That's when I made the big mistake. Instead of backing up my mother, I just gave Connie whatever it was she was currently demanding. The demands changed and grew in cost as Connie matured.

Over the years I dated a few women, but Connie hated them all, and I quickly gave into her temper tantrums by giving up the women. Things got worse when Connie was a senior in high school, and my folks retired and moved to Florida. With them gone, and Connie unable to maintain a relationship, I was the one who was pelted with her elitist demands. If I didn't give her what she wanted, the consequences shattered my nerves. It was so much easier to acquiesce to her than to live with her constant whining. When my folks left she made me sell our bungalow and buy a huge estate in Beverly Hills.

When Connie was a freshman in college, she came home for Thanksgiving holiday. The few weeks I lived alone after she left for the university, were the best of my life since she was born. I actually started seeing a woman, and the sex we had was stupendous. I couldn't wait to introduce the two women in my life to each other. I was certain that Connie would act differently now that she was a mature woman of eighteen.

It was not to be. Connie worked her black magic and the woman disappeared from my life in a day. She managed to do all this while bringing a new man home with her. Apparently she was allowed to have boyfriends, but I was forbidden to have girlfriends. Maybe she didn't want me spending my money on anyone else but her.

It turned out that her new friend was her English professor. He lived in Los Angeles and he too was home for the holiday. At the time, George Farmer PhD was thirty-two years old, I was thirty-eight and Connie was nineteen. George and I had more in common than he and Connie. We hit it off big time and Connie grew insanely jealous. After just three days, on the day before Thanksgiving, Connie gave George the boot for refusing to buy her some expensive bauble or other. I lost my girlfriend, and Connie eliminated another boyfriend in the space of three days.

Imagine how shocked I was when George called me on Thanksgiving Eve and asked me if I wanted to play tennis or golf with him Friday morning at The West Los Angeles Country Club where his folks had a membership. My golf game was non existent, and my tennis game was rusty so I opted for tennis. When I told George that I hadn't played tennis in quite a while, he told me that the club's tennis pro was giving a clinic at nine. He would arrange for us to attend the clinic, play afterward, and then have lunch at the club. I liked George a lot and really looked forward to spending the day with him.

Naturally when I told Connie that I was spending Friday with George, she had a temper tantrum to end all temper tantrums.

She packed her bags and took off to go back to school before we had our Thanksgiving together. You guessed it. She had cajoled me into buying her an expensive sport's car before she went off to the university, so there was nothing to stop her. I hate to admit it, but I was glad to see her go and I looked forward to my day with George.

Early Thanksgiving morning, I got another telephone call from George. He told me that he had spoken to Mark Cook, the tennis pro, and he would be glad to meet us Friday morning at 8 AM for a private lesson before the clinic. I was delighted and accepted immediately. George was nice enough to ask about Connie. When I told him she had gone back to school, he surprised me yet again.

"My folks went to the Bahamas for the holiday," he informed me. "Would you have Thanksgiving dinner with me at the club? I didn't want to eat alone and I wasn't going to celebrate the holiday at all, but if you would break bread with me, I'd be delighted." Again I accepted immediately.

"I'll call the club and reserve us a table," he said. "Thanks, Mr. Saunders," he added, "you've rescued my holiday."

"Please," I said my name is Albert. Call me Al."

George requested I meet him at the bar and that's where I was when he walked in. He shook my hand warmly and sat down next to me. The bartender came over to take his order.

"Dr. Farmer," the bartender said, "How nice to see you? It's been a couple of months now."

"Hi Jamie," George said. "I'd like you to meet my friend Al Saunders."

Jamie shook my hand and surprised me by winking at George. Now what was that all about?

"How's Daniel?" George asked Jamie.

"He's doing great. He graduates from fire fighter school in a couple of months. Now what can I give you?"

George gave him his order and Jamie took off. "Who's Daniel?" I asked.

"He's his partner. Jamie is gay. The whole thing is a water cooler story. Daniel is the son of a member of the club, and the former step son of the club's tennis pro. His two father's are gay also and they are now partners. The four of them go out together all the time."

The story was indeed shocking. "That's really civil of them," I muttered. "I can't wait to meet the pro tomorrow.

The dinner was excellent and the service was five-star. After dinner we went to the bar. After several drinks (and a warning from Jamie) we were both pretty sloshed. It was then that George made a suggestion. We couldn't know it at the time, but it was exactly at that moment that our lives became intertwined in a single defining historical occasion.

"I have a suggestion," George said. "Neither of us should drive. We've had too much to drink. Let's leave our cars here, and we'll take a cab home. You can stay over at my house. We have to be here so early tomorrow anyhow; we can come back together in the morning. I can lend you a tennis racket and some tennis clothes. We're about the same size."

"That's a wonderful idea," I said. "I never expected to drink so much. You must let me reimburse you."

"Forget about it. It's all charged to my father and he has to spend a minimum amount every month. Since he's away, it's better he pays for us than for nothing." That explanation more than satisfied my sense of ethics.

George asked Jamie to call us a cab, and we went outside to await its arrival. I don't know if I was more or less drunk than George, but I fell asleep in the cab with my head on George's shoulder. I vaguely remember George trying to undress me and get me into bed. A complete blackout followed. The next thing that I became aware of was bright sunshine coming into the room I had slept in. I estimated from the light that it was mid morning and that we had probably missed our tennis lessons and our tennis game. I had a throbbing headache and I didn't much care. I just went right back to sleep.

When I finally began to awaken, I froze. As I came to consciousness, I realized that George was in the bed with me. We were both naked, and George was nested up against me. I knew a stiff prick when I saw one, but now for the first time in my life I distinctly felt one pressing against my backside, pounding against my ass crack, trying to gain entry. George was snoring lightly. I know I should have jumped out of bed, but this all felt so good and so right, that I merely hunkered into the sleeping man and he pushed his stiff cock harder into me. I decided not to move as long as George didn't try to start something. I had no reason to believe he would, so why did the thought even cross my mind?

It seemed odd to me that I wasn't feeling strange about sleeping naked with another man. In fact, I was so relaxed I fell asleep again. When I finally awoke for good, I was alone in the bed. I had a huge boner and needed to pee badly. I ran to the bathroom naked, because I didn't know where my clothes were. After I relieved myself, I searched for my clothes, but they were nowhere to be found. Then I looked for a robe, but didn't find one.

The distinct odor of frying bacon invaded my nostrils and instinctively I followed the aroma and found myself approaching the kitchen. The kitchen table was set for two and George was at the stove. He was as naked as I was. Before he could notice me, I took a good look at him. Like me he stands 6'2" tall and we both weigh about 190 pounds. We both have brown hair and brown eyes. It occurred to me that maybe Connie was attracted to George because we actually resembled each other. Most important, his cock is just like mine also, about five inches flaccid, uncut and rather thick. We could pass as two brothers. Even our ages were right for brotherhood.

I stood transfixed staring at George's naked body. I found myself becoming aroused. My cock was rising, and by now I was no longer surprised that he was turning me on.

"Where are my clothes?" I asked, startling him.

"Good, you're up," he said. "I was just going to wake you. Breakfast is almost ready. Your socks, underwear and shirt needed freshening so I made a wash. Besides, I'm a bit of a naturist and I don't wear clothes around the house. Do you mind?"

"No, not at all," I answered. "You have a beautiful body which I am enjoying gazing at." What possessed me to say that?

"I'm blushing," George said. "Now get the orange juice out of the fridge and sit down at the table. The bacon and eggs will be ready in a second."

I was uncomfortable at first with our nudity, but I got over it quickly enough, and soon I was actually unaware of our state of undress. I reckoned that his penchant for nudity was the reason George was not shy about us sleeping naked together.

"I guess we can scratch tennis for today," I observed.

"Yes," George answered. "I've already called Mark and explained that we had too much to drink last night and I told him we'll take a rain check."

Changing the subject, George asked, "Did you find the bartender to be good looking? He's sleeping with Mark Cook's step son."

"I really didn't notice," I answered.

"Before Daniel moved in with him, I used to trick with him whenever I could. He's quite a lover."

For a moment I was too shocked to speak, but I regained my composure, and said a few things which I am sure sounded dumb. "I didn't know you were gay. Why were you dating my daughter? You must know that she's promiscuously heterosexual."

"Of course I knew. I never touched her. I would never get involved with a student anyway. Whatever relationship we might have had was a figment of her imagination."

I breathed a sigh of relief. Why? I don't know. I was just glad to hear that there was nothing between this guy and my daughter.

"Why did you sleep naked with me?" I blurted out without thinking.

"Because I like your body too. I enjoy sleeping cuddled up to another man. You were out like a light, so I didn't think you would notice or mind."

Again without thinking I said, "I didn't mind at all, even when I wasn't out like a light."

George's face suddenly lit up into an oversized grin. He reached across the table and put his hand on mine. "Can I interest you in the joys of gay sex?" he asked, and he curled a phantom mustache with the fingers of his other hand.

Without even a second's hesitation, I answered, "Yes, you sure can."

Without showing any further emotion, George said, "Eat your breakfast and then we'll shower together." Just then I heard my cell phone ringing. I heard it, but I had no idea where it was.

"That's my cell phone," I blurted out. "Do you know where it is?"

"Yes, I left it on the front hall table. I'll get it for you."

I opened the phone to a tirade (even worse than usual) from Connie. "Where are you?" she demanded to know. "I came home to an empty house and had to spend the night alone."

"I thought you had gone back to school," I said meekly. I should have told her that it was none of her business where I was, but old habits do indeed die hard. Connie intimidated me.

"When will you be home?" she screamed out at me.

"I don't know," I answered less meekly. "When I'm good and ready, I suppose." I hung up and powered off the phone.

"If you don't mind my saying so, I think your Connie needs to be taken down a few pegs," George observed.

"And just what did you have in mind?" I asked, indicating that I agreed with him, and would like a few suggestions.

"Did you ever read The Taming of The Shrew?" he asked. Well of course I had. "We need to devise a game plan to tame Connie. Keep in mind that it's for her own good," he concluded. "Let's talk about it later. For the moment, I promised to take you to paradise. Do you still want to go there?"

My stomach jumped a little, but I was anxious to find out why this great guy was arousing me so much. "Let's do it," I stated assertively.

I was totally surprised by what happened next. George took hold of my cock and fondled it. It rose to attention immediately. "Let's go," he said. Holding my cock, he led me up the stairs and into the master bathroom. He let go of me only to start the shower. The fact that he led me upstairs by my cock, and not by my arm, was so erotic to me that I almost came before we went into the shower.

George adjusted the water temperature to his liking. I knew that it would be perfect for me also. We just stood under the cascading water for a little while, staring at each other. Suddenly (and I do mean surprisingly suddenly) George wrapped his arms around me, and leaned in to kiss me. Considering that I had never kissed a man before, not even my father, I could not believe how quickly I responded. Our lips parted and we began to tickle each other's tongues. George's erection was pressed against mine and we began to rub our cocks together. God, it felt good.

George pulled away a little and I felt his hand engulf my prick. Somehow he had soaped up his hand and now he was massaging my cock with soap. I wanted to reciprocate, but I didn't know where the soap was at the moment. I felt so good that all I could do was close my eyes and sigh deeply. George stopped stroking my cock and turned me around. Now he rubbed his prick up and down my crack as he continued to stroke my soapy cock. I thought he might try to enter me. I would let him of course, but I was filled with fear. He let go of me without warning and fell to his knees. Now I felt a new sensation. Nobody had ever done to me what George was doing. He was rimming my ass and I wanted to scream with joy, but I muffled the noises coming out of me.

I felt fear again and even lost my erection for a little bit when I felt George's fingers penetrate my ass. I was happy that it didn't hurt. In fact it felt good, but then a second and a third finger entered me. I saw stars and was about to scream out and stop him, when his probing fingers touched a magic spot within me. The pain was still there, but lessening, as I felt a sensation that was so erotic, I felt that I was going to cum. I could feel the orgasm building deep within me.

I pulled away and yelled, "I'm cumming George, and I don't want to yet."

George stood up and embraced me. "Soap up your cock and fuck me," he said. I was amazed. He was asking me to perform an act which I considered totally intimate and he asked me to do it just exactly like he would ask me to turn on the TV. I didn't know where to start, but I followed his direction. He leaned against the shower wall and pushed out his butt to invite me to enter. I got my dick good and soapy and placed my head in his crack. He reached behind himself and took hold of my cock which he positioned at his opening.

"Push in slowly," he instructed and I did, or at least I tried. In spite of the fact that he was tighter than any cunt I had ever been in, I slipped in easily. For sure George had a well experienced ass hole. When I was all the way in, I didn't move at all. I was savoring how warm and comforting my cock felt buried in his ass. George began to move his hips and I began to thrust lightly. I was so horny and he was so tight that I felt the orgasm I was trying to delay coming on. There was no stopping it and George knew.

"Cum inside my ass," he yelled. "Please don't pull out." I couldn't have pulled out if I wanted to. It wasn't the best orgasm I ever had in my life. My position in the shower was pulling at my calf muscles, but it was an intense and satisfying one.

"Would you let me fuck you now?" George asked very meekly. How could I say no? I nodded, we kissed yet again, and George gave me my first fuck. It hurt when he entered me, but the pain was quickly replaced with extreme pleasure. All during the time he was in me, I felt like I might cum again, but I never did.

After the shower we lay naked in George's bed. We were hugging tightly and our limp dicks were touching. George was nibbling at my ear when he whispered in it. "How did you enjoy your first male sexual experience?"

I reflected a moment before answering. "I liked it enough to know that I want more, a lot more."

"Wait until I give you a blow job," George said. "You'll never let a woman do it to you again."

I laughed. "When will that be?" I asked.

"Soon, very soon," he laughed.

Actually we dozed off and he didn't blow me until at least five hours later. Now I can say that was the most intense orgasm I ever had. No woman had ever come close to satisfying me the way George did. When he asked me to do him, I almost balked, but I wouldn't let on, and decided to go for it. So far everything else had been so pleasurable. I tried to do everything he had done to me. From the sounds of his throat murmurings, I must brag and say that I was pretty sure I was satisfying him. It took a lot of will power to lick his dick head and then take him into me, but it tasted fresh scrubbed and perfumed and I really got into it after awhile. I even swallowed his cum as he had mine.

"How did I do"? I asked him.

"You did good, real good," he answered. He kissed me again and we started to doze off once more. I wasn't sure, but as we were falling asleep, I thought I heard George whisper, "I know what we have to do about taming your daughter," he said. "I'll tell you about it in the morning."

PART TWO

Connie was really worried now. Al had made good his threat. He hadn't been home for two days now. She had gone shopping without him and had maxed out her credit cards. She needed daddy to pay for her further indulgences. She didn't even have enough money to buy gas for the long drive back to school. She regretted having given George the boot.

Early Sunday morning, she heard a key turn the lock in the front door. "Daddy is that you?" she yelled in delight, and ran to the front hall. The door opened and there stood two men with guns drawn. They wore ski caps pulled down their faces with holes cut out for their eyes. They looked like monsters to Connie. She froze in place. She tried to scream, but before she could, one of the thugs covered her mouth. They dragged her out and into their car, carefully locking Al's front door. Connie started out by kicking and squirming, but somewhere along the line she passed out from fright and since she was light as a feather, she presented the kidnappers with no further trouble.

When she woke up she found herself tied tightly to a chair, and much to her dismay she was naked. Worse, the two abductors were similarly disrobed. The ski masks were off and Connie found them to be two very attractive men in their very early twenties. They both had better than average cut dicks, and that helped her relax a little about being naked. Neither of them was particularly tall, perhaps about 5'8". Connie felt certain that she could seduce them both.

"Who are you? What do you want? How did you get the key to my house?" she demanded to know. "If it's ransom you're after my father will pay anything to get me back."

The first man started to laugh. "What if he can't or won't meet our demands? What are you willing to do to rescue yourself?"

"He'll pay," she assured him. "He worships the ground I walk on. Is it my body you both want?" Connie smiled uncertainly at them. They both got hysterical with laughter.

"Your body is the last thing we want," the second man assured her. "Watch," he demanded, so Connie watched them. The two men embraced each other and started kissing. As they did so they began to fondle each other and their cocks began to rise. The first man fell to his knees and started to blow the second. The second man began to talk dirty, very dirty.

"Suck harder, cocksucker," he demanded of his mate. "Take my hot rod down your throat and suck me dry." Connie was appalled. She had never heard such language. The man got more and more obscene the closer he got to his climax. Suddenly he pulled out of his friend's mouth and faced Connie. He finished himself off and covered Connie's face and breast with thick, creamy, plentiful cum.

Connie screamed, "Clean me off you scum. I'll see to it that you both go to prison for years when I get free."

"I guess we won't ever be able to let her go free then," the first man said. Connie grew pale and she sickened at the thought.

"You know," the second man said, "that wonderful blow job you gave me has made me hungry. Let's eat something." He went to the fridge and brought back a sleeve of white bread and some sliced roast beef. He made two sandwiches, garnished the meat with mustard, and offered one to his co-conspirator.

"I'm starving," Connie said. "Make me a sandwich." The two men ignored her.

"Did you hear any magic words?" the first man asked. The second shook his head.

"I'm hungry," Connie persisted.

"Still no magic," the second man said.

They finished eating, and number two put everything back in the fridge. He removed two cans of beer and the pair began to consume their drinks.

"I'm thirsty," Connie declared. The men ignored her.

"I need to pee," she declared further.

"You'll pee when we tell you to. If you can't wait, feel free to let loose all over yourself."

For the first time, Connie's face showed some concern. She knew she couldn't sway them with sex, so she hoped maybe she could win them over by befriending them.

"My name is Constance," she told them.

"Tell us something we don't know," the second man said.

"Well you know my name. What do I call you two hot studs?"

"Flattery won't work," the first man said, "but if you must know, my name is Tim and this here's Bertie, short for Burton."

"Pleased to meet you," Connie said facetiously. "Look, I really have to pee."

"Hold it in," Tim said showing no pity." Then the first miracle happened. Connie began to cry, not crocodile tears reserved for whining and begging, but real honest to goodness tears of discomfort.

"See that clock on the wall," Tim continued. "It's 9:45. When the big hand is on the twelve and the little hand is on the eleven, you can pee, not a second before. Now, we would like to talk to your father about ransom. Give us his cell phone number."

Bertie went into another room to make the call, and he closed the door behind him. He came out after five minutes and he was laughing so hard, he couldn't talk.

"How much did you ask for and what did he say?" Connie asked. She still hadn't said the magic word so Bertie ignored her. He looked at Tim and said, "Houston, we have a problem."

"Tell me," Tim begged.

"Her father said he would pay us twice as much to keep her. He said she was so costly, it would be worth every penny he gave us because he figures he'll be a near millionaire by the end of the year."

"I never expected that," Tim said. "What should we do?"

"Maybe he'll be more sympathetic to our demands if we tell him that we are going to torture her, but we want the ransom, and he has to take her back," Bertie said. He looked at Connie. "I can see why he doesn't want you back," he said.

"You're wrong," she said. "My father loves me. I'll bet you never spoke to him."

"Oh yes I did," Bertie retorted. "He's with a Dr. Farmer. Does that mean anything to you?" Connie slumped in her chair.

"I need to pee," she repeated, "and I need to wipe your cum off my face."

Tim informed Bertie that he had not yet heard the magic word which might open the bathroom door, and so they ignored her. Finally Tim said, "It's my turn and you know what I mean." He sat down on a chair. Bertie got on his knees and began to suck Tim's cock in plain view of Connie. While he was getting a great BJ from his pal, Tim asked Connie if she ever did this to a man.

"Never," she replied. "It's disgusting."

"No wonder you can't keep a man," he replied. "Would you like us to teach you how? You can practice on us."

For a second Connie thought that going down on her captors might buy her release, but she wasn't certain so instead she said, "Fuck off."

Tim was about to say, "Tsk, tsk," but he started to cum and he screamed out obscenities instead.

"Disgusting," Connie reiterated.

"Disgusting indeed!" Tim said when he could breathe again. "The only thing disgusting is you. You wish it was your mouth I just came in. Admit it."

"Pig," was all Connie could spit out.

"Hey girl," Bertie said, "It's yours when you want it."

Just then there was a knock on the door. Bertie opened it and in walked another young man in his early twenties. Connie's jaw dropped open. She had never seen anyone so handsome in her life. He looked like a Greek statue. He was over six feet tall. He had black curly hair, cut short. His eyes were deep blue, and they offset his pale complexion. He had a straight Roman nose, a square jaw, and about a day's growth of beard. There was something vaguely familiar about him. She thought for a moment that she might know him, but she couldn't place him. As for the young man he took one look at Connie and did a double take, presumably dazzled by her beauty.

"Tim and I have things to do so Jimmy here is taking over for us," Bertie said. "You better be nicer to him than you have been to us. He has a reputation for beating up on women." Jimmy said nothing. He glared at Connie and started to undress while Tim and Bertie got dressed to leave. As he locked the door behind them, Jimmy spoke for the first time.

"Let's get the rules straight," he said. "While we wait for the ransom, you can be comfortable or very, very uncomfortable. It's strictly your choice to make."

Connie didn't know what to say so she kept her mouth shut for a change.

Jimmy continued. "I am the only one making demands around here. You will always do everything I ask you to do. You will not question my authority. If you need something, you will ask pleasantly and you will say PLEASE. Otherwise I will not do as you ask. Do you understand?"

Connie wasn't sure where this was heading so she just nodded. By now Jimmy was fully undressed and Connie was fully aroused. She could not take her eyes off his cock. It was the biggest she had ever seen, at least six flaccid, cut inches. It was hefty as well and his balls were full and succulent. As far as Connie was concerned things were looking up. She could only wonder if Jimmy was straight and if she could seduce him.

"I need to pee badly," she told him. "If I don't get to the bathroom soon, you won't like what will happen."

"So?" Jimmy asked.

"So take me to the bathroom."

"You don't listen too well. I gave you specific instructions which you have disobeyed. For that you have to stroke my cock with your tongue. Don't try to bite me. You won't like the consequences if you do." He approached her and held his cock out in front of her mouth. She stroked the underside once with her tongue. Jimmy got an instant erection. At least he's straight, she reasoned.

"Now what was it you wanted?" he asked.

"I need to pee," she said stubbornly.

"And?"

"Please, please take me to the bathroom."

"Of course, I will. Now wasn't that easy?"

He untied her from the chair and she was surprised to find that her hands were tied behind her with a separate rope. She stood and ran toward the bathroom. The seat was up and she turned to look at Jimmy. Lower the seat," she snapped, "before I die."

"Obey the rules or pee with the seat up," he answered.

"PLEASE," she begged, and Jimmy lowered the seat.

She didn't care that the door was open and Jimmy watched her pee. She was eliminating water in a torrent. Jimmy approached her and put his cock to her mouth. "You lapsed again, and I had to remind you to say please," he said. "For that you will give me another lick or two as punishment."

"Why don't you say please?"

"I told you, I make the demands anyway I want to. You make them politely."

"OK, I get it," she whimpered. "I'm very hungry. Could you please, pretty please, give me something to eat when I'm through here?"

"Cut the sarcasm if you know what's good for you."

Connie nodded meekly. "How can I wipe myself?" she asked. "My hands are tied behind me."

"I'll do it for you," Jimmy said. He took a wad of toilet paper and dabbed lightly at her Venus entrance. He was so gentle that Connie got completely turned on. "Let's see if I did a good job, he said. He leaned down and kissed Connie gently on her clitoris. She thought she would swoon.

Jimmy sat her at the kitchen table. He made her a roast beef sandwich and poured her a coke. He refused to untie her hands and he fed her instead. Connie was mortified, but there wasn't much she could do about it."

When she was finished eating, Jimmy started to tie her to the chair again. "Please," she cried, "the chair is so uncomfortable. Couldn't you at least tie me to a bed?"

Jimmy smiled at her. "See how easy it's getting. You said please, so your wish is my command." He put her in a twin size bed and tied each ankle to the foot posts. Then he untied her hands and tied each wrist to the head posts. She was more comfortable now, but she was lying on her back fully exposed to him. She was so turned on, her vagina was oozing and fluid was leaking down her leg. Jimmy noticed and he began to yearn for what appeared to be a fountain of love.

"I'm going to make love to you," he said. "I'm not asking you, I'm demanding, and you have no choice." Connie was stunned, but she wanted him badly and simply nodded. In fact they were both so hot and needy, that Jimmy bypassed all foreplay. He lay on top of her, and entered her easily. Unfortunately he neglected to use a condom.

Jimmy came once and Connie came three times. He released her ties and the two lay in the bed together wrapped up in each other's arms. Connie was weeping.

"Why are you crying?" Jimmy asked.

"This is the craziest thing," she moaned. "I love you. Isn't that weird? I knew the moment you walked in the room that you wouldn't hurt me, and that I had nothing to fear from you. Tim and Bertie didn't really frighten me either. They seem like two little cupcakes to me."

"Connie, Connie," Jimmy said. "I have yearned for you ever since the first time I saw you on campus. I can't lie to you anymore. My name is Philip Watson."

Connie's eyes lit up. "I know you," she said. "You're majoring in drama. I saw you in a play that the drama department put on, *Rosencrantz and Guildenstern Are Dead*. Tim and Bertie played the title characters and you were Hamlet. If I remember correctly Dr. Farmer directed the play."

"That's right," Philip said.

"If you were so stricken by me?" Connie asked, "Why didn't you try to meet me and to date me?"

"I love you Connie, but you know you have a terrible reputation. Everyone knows that you only go for wealthy guys who can indulge your whims. I'm a poor student. I have great potential, but I can't offer you anything but my love for the time being."

Connie began to cry. "Forgive me," she said, "PLEASE forgive me. Right now, I don't want anything more in the world than you." They kissed passionately and began to make love again. They made love all night.

In the morning, Philip gave Connie her clothes and they both got dressed. Once again they kissed passionately. "Come," Philip said, "I'll explain everything and take you to your father."

PART THREE

When George and I woke up from having made love for what seemed like a dozen times, George said, "Let's talk about Connie. She's not a very nice person and she's spoiled rotten."

"I guess I indulged her too much," I admitted. "You mentioned something about having a plan to tame her," I reminded him.

"Yes. I not only teach English, I head up the drama department. I know any number of budding actors. Many of them live here in LA. How about I engage a few of them for an acting gig? We know that Connie is back home and she can't leave because she has no money. Let one of these boys stage a mock kidnapping, and he can do like Petruchio. The funny thing is that we have started to rehearse for Taming of The Shrew to be presented before Christmas break. The actors can rehearse on Connie. Too bad I've already cast Katherina. Connie could play the part with a lot of conviction."

"They wouldn't harm her, would they? I wouldn't want her hurt in any way."

"They wouldn't harm her at all," George said. "They would just make her miserable like Petruchio made Kate."

"I'm not sure about this," I said. "I just know that something has to be done to make her into a real human being. I'm willing to give it a try."

George went to his Blackberry and retrieved some telephone numbers. He called each one in turn, and asked them to be at his house at noon. He told them that he would take them to lunch and offer them an acting gig.

"Why three?" I asked. "All we need is one."

"I figure one or two might turn us down. It's for insurance."

Tim and Bertie arrived in one car and Phil arrived moments later in a separate car. Introductions were made. They were all good looking, but I wouldn't mind furthering my gay education in Philip's arms. He was gorgeous, but very straight. Then again, who knew? I thought I was straight also until I fell head over heels in love with George. Best thing yet; I think George felt the same way. We all transferred to George's car and headed for the country club.

While we were waiting for a table we went to the bar. Now I was much more aware of things. Jamie ogled the three handsome men, but he flipped over Philip, and who could blame him? Just before we were called to our table, Mark Cook walked through the bar. George called to him and introduced us all. God he was handsome. I was surrounded by handsome men. I almost regretted that I missed my lesson with Mark, but what George and I did instead was much more satisfying.

At lunch, George described Connie's extraordinary beauty and I could see that Philip's interest was peaked. Not so much Tim and Bertie. Then he went on to tell them that she was a real live Kate, a shrew of the first order. He described his plan to tame her and advised the men that they could employ similar tactics as in the play. They all laughed and said that they were up for the challenge. It was agreed to use Phil's apartment as the other two men still lived with their parents. They took my address and left to convene at Phil's house to lay out their game plan, which they wanted to put into effect the following morning.

When they left, I looked at George. "You know," I told him, "I'm anxious for more lessons. Are you up to it?"

"I'm a healthy homosexual male who has fallen madly in love with the father of one of my students. I'm more than up to it, so let's get out of here."

We couldn't get out of there fast enough and back into George's shower. "OK," George said jokingly, "before we get into advanced technique, let's review your first few lessons."

He fell to his knees and started rimming my ass. Suddenly, I burst into tears. My body was racked with huge spasms as I sobbed uncontrollably. George jumped up and encircled me with his strong arms. "What's the matter?" he asked me. "Please don't cry."

"Nothing is wrong," I reassured him. "It's just that I'm so damned happy. I haven't been this happy ever in my life. Please, love, make us one body. Fuse as together. Get inside of me as far as you can and never get out." George kissed me and laughed.

"I wish I could stay inside of you forever, but I'll do my best to stay in as long as I can."

"Please," I said, "let's dry up and take this to the bedroom."

This started a non stop sex regime that I never wanted to end. I found it difficult to let go of George. I just wanted to hold him and have him hold me tight. Somehow I needed the reassurance that I was loved.

We were interrupted twice. Shortly after lunch on Sunday, Tim and Bertie called to let us know that Connie was fine, but they were being hard on her by ignoring her demands until she could bring herself to say, please. So far, she hadn't said it and she had no idea what they wanted when they referred to "the magic word."

The next day was Monday. I called the office to say I wouldn't be in that day. George and I remained entwined until the phone rang at about 9 AM. We were shocked to hear Phil's voice.

"I've had enough of the game," he said. "I'm bringing Connie home now. Shall I bring her to her home or yours, Dr. Farmer?"

"Hold on a minute," George said. He filled me in and I told him to tell Phil to come here. "I want her to know about us," I told George. "If she doesn't like it, well that's just tough shit."

George kissed me and said, "That's my boy."

When Phil and Connie came into the house, I felt that something had changed in my daughter. She ran to me and kissed me and cried on my shoulder. I figured she was crying about her recent ordeal.

"Why are you crying?" I asked.

"I'm crying because I'm so happy," she said. (Like father, like daughter.) "I'm in love, Daddy," she went on, "With Phil. He doesn't know where he's going to get tuition for his next semester. He can't offer me a thing, but I love him. Please, please, Dad. I won't ever ask you for another thing for myself, but will you please help Phil?"

I never really answered her question. I just hugged her so tightly she had to get my meaning. Now I had to tell her about George and me. I didn't know how, so I just blurted out, "Honey, I'm in love also. I found the one person I want to spend the rest of my life with and be buried beside. I really don't care if you disapprove, this one is a keeper and I'm keeping HIM."

"Him?" Connie asked aghast.

"Him?" Phil asked aghast.

"Yes," George piped in, "it's me and I feel the same way about your father. I want to spend the rest of my life with him."

Finally Connie found her voice. "Well you better not ever hurt him," she said, "or you'll have to answer to Phil and me."

A few weeks later, just before Christmas, I found myself in the audience at the University Drama Club's production of Shakespeare's The Taming of The Shrew. Connie sat to my right and George sat next to her. She squeezed both our hands every time Phil came on stage. I really did not expect to see the production I saw. Amateur productions are a definite turn off for me.

I guess I never told you what I do for a living. I'm a film producer. Not just any film producer. I have three Oscars and an Emmy to my name and I'm far from done. I have worked with the best actors this world has produced, so it is no idle statement to say that my future son in law, Phil, blew me away. His performance transfixed and mesmerized me. His fellow actors were wonderful, but he was superb. In the end it was totally believable that Katherina would succumb to his authority, and want to be the best wife ever, just to please him.

At this time, I was in pre-production for a romantic comedy. The average public thinks that such movie fare is fluff. In truth, the genre is a huge challenge for an actor. The plots are usually predictable and sometimes absurd. It takes a good actor to convince the public of the reality of the situation. I had already signed the female lead. She was famous, popular, beautiful and talented. She would draw the crowds all by herself. I knew I could afford to take a chance on a fresh new face for the male lead, and I found him playing Petruchio that evening.

Phil is rich and famous now. In spite of that, Connie never asks him for a thing. She doesn't have to. He buys her anything he sees that he thinks she might like. Connie has devoted her life to making him and my two grandsons a happy home.

Speaking of happy homes, George now teaches at UCLA and we live together in luxury as well. We would be happy together if we didn't have a pot to pee in. We may not make love every single day anymore, but we love each other more and more every day. I have even lately been toying with the idea of making a movie, a romantic comedy if you will, about a gay couple. The usual religious fanatics will probably picket the theaters, but I can afford a loss to get the message out.

About the Author

Hank Brooks was born in Brooklyn, NY and lived most of his adult life in and around the New York City area.

He is very active in SAGE, a senior advocacy group for gay men and women.

He has three children and five grandsons. He is a retired CPA, and now lives with his partner, Leo, in Coconut Creek, Florida.

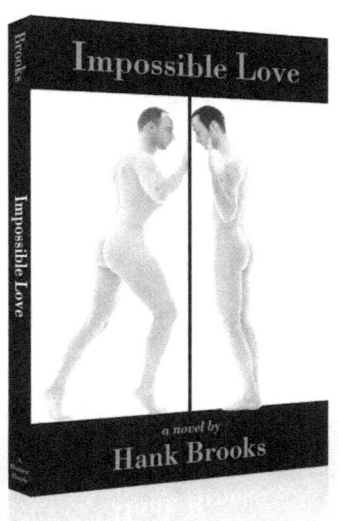

www.ingramcontent.com/pod-product-compliance
Lightning Source LLC
Chambersburg PA
CBHW051126260626
47170CB00005B/1679